TOWARDS A MENAGERIE

Also by David Miller

Art and Disclosure: Seven Essays, Stride, Exeter, 1998

Commentaries, tel-let, Charleston, IL, 1999

Commentaries (II), Runaway Spoon Press, Port Charlotte, FL, 2000

The Waters of Marah: Selected Prose 1973-1995, Shearsman Books, Exeter, 2005

The Dorothy and Benno Stories, Reality Street Editions, Hastings, 2005

British Poetry Magazines 1914-2000: A History and Bibliography of 'Little Magazines' (with Richard Price), The British Library, London / Oak Knoll Press, New Castle, DE, 2006

Spiritual Letters (Series 1-5), Chax Press, Tucson, 2011

Black, Grey and White: A Book of Visual Sonnets, Veer Books, London, 2011

A River Flowing Beside, hawkhaven press, San Francisco, 2013

Reassembling Still: Collected Poems, Shearsman Books, Bristol, 2014

Spiritual Letters (Series 6), Shearsman Books, 2015

From Late to Early [e-book], otata's bookshelf, 2017

Edited by David Miller

The ABCs of Robert Lax (with Nicholas Zurbrugg), Stride, 1999

Music while drowning: German Expressionist Poems (with Stephen Watts), Tate Publishing, London, 2003

The Lariat and other writings by Jaime de Angulo, Counterpoint, Berkeley, 2009

The Alchemist's Mind: a book of narrative prose by poets, Reality Street, 2012

The Narcosis of Water by David Menzies, Poetry Salzburg, Salzburg, 2017

Collected Poems by James Harvey (with Antony John and Keith Jebb), Veer Books, 2017

Towards a Menagerie:
Eight Stories

David Miller

chax / tucson / 2019

ISBN 978-1-946104-17-5

Chax Press books are supported in part by a fund at the University of Houston-Victoria, and largely by individual donors. Please visit *https://chax.org/membership-support/* if you would like to contribute to our mission to make an impact on the literature and culture of our time.

Chax Press
1517 North Wilmot Road #264
Tucson, Arizona 85712-4410
USA

Press Acknowledgments: Chax Press would like to acknowledge the assistance of our artistic consultant, Cynthia Miller, on the design of this book, and our UHV intern, Ashley Kilday, for assistance with manuscript preparation, layout, and proofreading.

Author Acknowledgments: These stories were written between 2013 and 2017. Several friends looked at them for me and made helpful comments: I am very much in their debt. Thanks also to Ken White for his paintings inspired by 'Freddy and Ian', one of which is reproduced here. Thanks to Lou Rowan, also, for publishing 'Jay and the Flamingo' in his magazine *Golden Handcuffs Review*.

Publisher's Note: In instances where the author's punctuation differs from standard American punctuation, such as the placement of commas or periods inside or outside of single or double quotation marks, we have followed the author's punctuation.

Painting on cover: Freddy no. 1, by Ken White.
Drawing on title page by David Miller.

to Dodo, with love

*FREDDY AND IAN, WHO SAILED
ACROSS THE SEA ON A RAFT*

Freddy lived in a place called Darwin, in the Northern Territory – at the top end of Australia. He'd lived there all his life. At various times he stayed with people in their houses, wherever he felt welcome – with *friends*, in other words. Once he also stayed in a boat; and this led to him taking a voyage across the sea on a raft, in the company of a painter named Ian. This is how it happened.

One day when Freddy was out and about, there'd been rain earlier, and now leaves slowly dripped water, and warm sunlight shone through the branches. He carried on down to the shore, until he came to a large boat, the kind that's known as a patrol boat. It had been left on the shore and was in such a bad condition that no one would have wanted it. Or so Freddy thought. This could be my new home, he said to himself.

When Freddy went inside, he was taken aback. He saw that not only was there a mattress and some plates and cups, but there were also paintings! He'd seen a few paintings before, during his many stays with friends, but seeing so many, and resting against the walls rather than hanging on them.... Could there be an artist living in the boat?

Freddy didn't know a great deal about paintings, but he could see that these were very good indeed – wonderful, in fact. He looked and looked.

He was surprised by someone behind him exclaiming: 'Why, it's a mouse!'

'I am certainly not!' said Freddy indignantly, as he turned around.

And he wasn't, though it's true he'd been mistaken for one before. If you were looking at him carefully, as the man now was, you'd see that he had a rather long head that became more and more slender until it ended at the point of the nose, and large black eyes. His tail was very long and stood upright. If you looked even more carefully, you might see that he had a pouch – a sort of pocket in his skin, like koalas and kangaroos have.

The man had been shocked into silence by Freddy's words. 'You can *talk*!' he finally said.

'Well, so can *you*!' Freddy replied.

'But I'm a human, I'm supposed to. Whereas you, you're a – a – '

'Antechinus', said Freddy. 'Ant-e-chin-us. Yes, I know... it's a mouthful.' He sighed. 'That's one reason why we get called pouched mice, even though we're not mice at all. I *look* a little like a mouse, so people think I *am* a mouse. Actually, I don't happen to like mice. None of my friends are mice. For one thing, mice have very poor manners. What do mice do when they're in your home and they see you?'

'They run away.'

'That's right. But that's not what we do. We make contact. We sit and look at you; we make sure you see us, and that we can feel that we're welcome. As well as being friendlier than a mouse, I'm also better looking.... I could go on and on about this. Let's just say I'm *preferable* to a mouse.'

'Do you normally *talk* to people?'

'Well, no. This is an exception. Consider yourself favoured. By the way, I like your paintings very much.'

'Thank you. My name's Ian. What's yours?'

'Freddy.'

Ian had bright blue eyes, and spoke with a soft Scottish accent. He had a gentle way about him. Freddy liked him immediately. From that time on, Freddy and Ian lived in the patrol boat together. Ian painted, while Freddy watched. He would often yell when he was painting. Freddy wasn't tempted to try to join in; he just sat and watched and listened. At other times he hunted for insects, or he sat and talked with Ian.

Ian liked to give people good wine, when he could afford it, which he served in empty peanut butter jars. But Freddy didn't drink. Only a very little water, and occasionally a little milk. (This was to prove useful later on.)

During their talks together, Freddy learned that Ian had lived in various parts of the world, including Scotland, England, Canada and even China. He'd once been on an island called Bali, in Indonesia. There he'd seen dancers in strange masks and clothes, and little girls who danced with wonderful grace in beautiful costumes. There was music everywhere – music that he found quite extraordinary and which it was easy to come to love. And people were friendly, but they left you alone when that's what you wanted. He'd felt at peace there.

Freddy dreamt that Ian would one day translate a Chinese book, the life of a holy man who loves drinking wine but is still very holy. Ian dreamt that Freddy would also translate a Chinese book. (This didn't actually happen, nor was it likely to have. Not all dreams come true, after all.)

Ian talked a good deal to Freddy about China, but he talked even more about Bali. One day Ian said, 'I can't see how I can get back to Bali from here, but I think I can get to Timor, which isn't too far from Bali. I think it might be as good a place as Bali, in fact!'

'How would you do that?' asked a surprised Freddy. He couldn't believe that Ian had enough money to go by ship. What was he doing living in an abandoned boat if he had money?

'Look, Freddy, here we are in Darwin – the coast is right on the Timor Sea – and the Timor Sea goes all the way to Timor! I just need to build a raft and I can sail there. It should only take about ten days, if there are good winds. Why don't you come along?'

At first, Freddy wasn't impressed. 'This is crazy, Ian', he said. 'You'd never make it! And there are crocodiles in the water along the coast, remember!'

'Don't be a scaredy cat antechinus', said Ian. 'I'm not afraid of crocodiles – and I'll protect you from them if necessary.'

Freddy, needless to say, didn't like being called a "cat" – cats were his enemies, because they hunted after him. His fur bristled and his tail twitched.

'Oh, all right then! I guess it will be an adventure.... How are you going to build this raft, anyway?'

Ian built the raft while Freddy watched. It took several days, and most of the material was found on the beach or on rubbish dumps. Ian used logs, planks and three old airplane fuel tanks, bound together with rope and wire. There was a wooden mast with a sail of parachute silk. The raft was in the shape of a triangle, and it was so small that Ian couldn't stand upright on it without it being tipped off balance. He would have to spend the entire time lying outstretched or sitting.

He nailed a little board to the raft and then built a tiny hut on it for Freddy. He knew that he had to keep Freddy safe, and he also wanted Freddy to be comfortable. Freddy could come out when the sea was calm and run along the planks and logs, but much of the time he would need to stay in his hut.

Ian took on board some tinned food, bottled water and a blanket. He also helped Freddy collect a supply of insects to last the voyage.

Finally the time came when it was all ready, and that evening Freddy hopped on board and went inside his hut (he was still worried about crocodiles), while Ian pushed the raft out into the water and managed – with quite some difficulty – to pull himself onto the raft without turning it over. Ian began to row with the oars, and the waves carried it further and further out.

On the second day of their voyage, they were spotted by a large fishing boat. The fishermen didn't seem to notice Freddy. However, they called out to Ian, asking him if he'd been shipwrecked, and did he want to be rescued. (The raft must have looked very odd to them, especially as the silk sail had already become torn in several places.), 'No', said Ian, 'I'm all right; but can you tell me if I'm going in the right direction for Timor?' They replied that he was, and then they continued on their way, shaking their heads in amazement....

As careful as Ian had been, the voyage was still frightening at times for Freddy – and for Ian himself as well. They were followed by sharks from time to time. Seabirds began to perch on the raft. Ian didn't like the sharks. Freddy didn't like either the birds or the sharks.

On the fifth day out, Ian had a strange experience which he described to Freddy. There seemed to be something like an enormous mosquito net stretching from the sky down to the sea. Stars shone through it at night. Figures – outlines of people – danced across it, and other figures danced behind them.

'Can you see them, Freddy?'

'No, Ian, I can't.'

This was of course worrying for Freddy. But things got worse.

There was a storm which lasted three days and nights. Freddy and Ian feared the entire time that the raft would turn over and they would drown, but it didn't. Ian, who tied his ankles to the mast so that he wouldn't be washed overboard, was drenched by the rain and the waves. Freddy kept to his hut; he didn't come out at all until the storm had let up.

The voyage took longer than Ian had thought it would. They ran out of food and water. The lack of water affected Freddy less than it did Ian. But the lack of food affected them equally.

On the fourteenth day they sighted the coast of Timor. But even though he tried, Ian couldn't guide the raft to the shore where he could attempt to land it. So to their dismay they just drifted parallel to the island for the next two days.

By the evening of the sixteenth day, stronger waves had carried the raft to a tiny nearby island called Roti, and a wave washed them up on the moonlit beach.

'We've arrived!' exclaimed Freddy. He could make out a town a little ways off, and hills in the distance.

But Ian collapsed on the sand in exhaustion. Freddy also felt terribly tired, and he went to sleep.

Freddy was woken by shouts and the sound of scuffling. To his horror, he saw that a group of policemen – or at least they looked like police, with their uniforms and guns – had surrounded Ian and bound him, and were now taking him away. Despite his hunger and weakness, Freddy followed as fast as he could.

However, Freddy was simply too exhausted. He had to sit and rest, and watch his friend being taken away, further and further into the distance.

It took Freddy several days to find Ian again. Having seen his friend arrested, he had no wish to be caught himself. So he was very careful, and less friendly with humans than usual. He just didn't want to take any chances. He searched in house after house, until he came to one with a policeman standing in front of it, carrying a gun, and he knew he'd found the right one. (At the same time, he found it hard to believe anyone would think Ian needed to be guarded by a man with a gun.) He crept around the back and slipped through a crack and into the house.

'Hello, Ian', whispered Freddy.

'Oh my God, you've found me', whispered Ian.

Ian told Freddy that the people of Roti thought he was some kind of a spy. Who else but a spy would arrive on their island on a raft, they said. Ian had replied that an artist would. They were not convinced.

'You have to help me, Freddy. I don't know what they're going to do with me! Can you somehow get back to Australia? If you could take a message from me, someone might be able to find a way of getting me released!'

Freddy thought he could do it.

So Ian tried to write a message as small as possible on a tiny scrap of paper that could be put in Freddy's pouch.

They shook their heads at each other. The paper was too large to fit into Freddy's pouch, unless Ian wrote the message in such a tiny handwriting that it was impossible to read or even recognise as a message. It wouldn't work. But Freddy knew what the message was. They also had to give up on the idea of Freddy going to several houses – Freddy couldn't remember all the names and addresses. So Ian decided on one person – an artist named Maie, whose husband worked for the Australian government. He wrote the name and address down so that Freddy could remember it.

'Weird!' said Freddy. 'What sort of a name is that? How do you say it?'

'Mai-e. It's not weird, it's just different. OK, don't worry about how to say it. Just get the message to her. And what sort of a name is "antechinus"?'

'I get the point', said Freddy.

So Freddy and Ian said goodbye to each other. Freddy knew what he had to do. As soon as he was able he sneaked on board a ship (he had no money for the fare, after all), and then another ship. He relied on what he heard Australians and Europeans – tourists, mainly – say to each other at the ports about where the ships were going. Eventually he arrived back in Australia, and after more travelling he found himself at Maie's home in East Melbourne, in Victoria. It hadn't been easy for Freddy; he'd had to hide away in trains and cars, picking up on what he overheard people say to plan his journey. Freddy was brave as well as smart, and he didn't give up. It was not something that an antechinus usually attempted, mind you. However, it wasn't usual for an antechinus to sail across the sea on a raft, either.

Freddy slipped through a crack into Maie's studio. She was standing in front of a painting, with a brush in her hand. Suddenly she became aware of Freddy's presence and turned around.

'Oh, it's a mouse!' she exclaimed.

'No, I'm *not*', said Freddy, and sighed. 'If you look carefully you'll see I'm not a mouse at all. I'm *better* than a mouse. But don't let's worry about that – I have something important to tell you.'

'You can *talk*!'

'Well, so can you! Now, please, just listen – this is about my painter friend, Ian; he's in trouble...'

....

Ian had been shipped from island to island. It didn't make any sense to him. But wherever he went, he was still kept as a prisoner, so one place really seemed no better than another.

He repeatedly said to his guards: 'I'm a painter. Please let me have some brushes and paints.'

'How can you be a painter? You're a spy!' he was told.

He missed Freddy and wondered what he was doing. He also wondered if Freddy had been able to reach Maie.

Then Ian was sent to Singapore. He didn't know why. It wasn't much better there: although no longer under arrest, he still wasn't free. He was forced to stay in a home for people who had no money and were not thought able to make a living. He felt miserable. He liked to be free – free to go wherever he wanted, and free to paint.

'I'm a painter, please let me have paints and brushes', he said one day.

'How can you be a painter? You're a man with no money!' came the reply.

(Ian could well have responded that painters are often people who have little or no money, but he didn't bother.)

When Maie eventually learned that Ian was in Singapore, she said to her husband: 'Richard, you must find a way for Ian to return to Australia! I've heard he's in some horrible place in Singapore where they won't even let him paint.'

Richard did everything he could. But things don't always turn out as you think they should. Ian was sent to England instead! That wasn't any stranger than having been sent from island to island in Southeast Asia, however.

Ian didn't feel at home in London, which is where he stayed while he was in England. True, he was no longer under arrest or forced to stay in a place he didn't want to, and he could paint if he felt like it. But he didn't want to be there, and he didn't even feel like painting. He missed Australia. Not that there was anything wrong with London – he guessed he had just become used to how things were and how things looked in Australia.

He still missed Freddy, but he'd begun to think that he might not see Freddy again for some while, at least. The place that kept coming into Ian's mind was Bribie Island, a tiny island off the coast of Queensland. He'd stayed there almost ten years before, and he'd thought it beautiful and... *friendly*. He wasn't really thinking of the people. The place itself seemed friendly, somehow. There was so much about it he'd liked. The sandy beaches, the beautiful blue sea waters, the clumps of trees, the magnificent evening skies... these were some of the things he remembered. He also remembered the animals – emus and kangaroos, especially – and the many different kinds of birds. Ian had felt at home there, and he wondered now why he'd ever left.

He went to see a wealthy relative who was living in London. He said: 'I can't paint here. I need to be back in Australia. Can you help me?'

The relative gave him some money towards his fare, and this made Ian decide to write to another of his relatives and ask the same thing, and then write to another. He soon had enough money for the journey. For the time being, he was no longer a poor person.

When Ian arrived back in Australia, it was Sydney where he landed, in New South Wales, and from there he made his way to Brisbane, in Queensland. He sailed over to Bribie Island, where he built himself a hut. Bribie Island was to be his home for the rest of his life. It was where he felt *at home*. He didn't go to Darwin again, or anywhere else in the Northern Territory.

In the meanwhile, Freddy had managed to make his way back to Darwin, sneaking on board trains and cars. He missed Ian. He heard nothing about what was happening with him, but he knew he had done his best to help him.

Freddy looked for a new home. Somehow he didn't really feel like returning to the patrol boat. After a week or so of searching, he found a house where he felt welcome – where, in other words, he had *friends*. Nicola and Tom, the young couple who lived there, always made a fuss of him whenever they saw him, and after a while they made a tiny hammock for him in their back garden. He could hunt for insects in the kitchen or in the garden, and he could sit in the living room while his friends talked, ate their meals, listened to music or played chess. Freddy didn't play chess, though he liked to watch. And as much as he enjoyed being with his new friends, he didn't feel like talking. He rarely did: only when he *really* wanted to, or else needed to. Ian and Maie had been exceptions. As it happened, Freddy really preferred to silently enjoy things, on the whole. It was only when he realised he was with a rare person like Ian, or when he needed to help someone like Ian, that he would speak.

Nicola and Tom had some paintings in their home, but Freddy didn't honestly think they were anywhere near as good as Ian's. Freddy would never know that Ian eventually became one of the most famous painters in Australia. However, he would not have been surprised.

This is the reason why.

On the first day when he'd sat looking at Ian's paintings in the patrol boat, Freddy had known that Ian would become a great artist.

The paintings in front of him were strange and beautiful, and they'd made him feel quite odd, in a way he liked. There were lines and there were patches of colour, and sometimes there weren't even any details of things, like people or trees or hills – there were just lines and colours. Not only that, but at times the colours and lines seemed to go in different ways, rather than a line simply wrapping itself around a patch of colour. Freddy had never seen anything like this! What had it felt like when he looked at them? Watching a thunderstorm from a dry place might have been one way of thinking about the sort of feeling he got from some of them. Other paintings had given him an extraordinary sense of calm, quiet and harmony – as if he were sitting in a forest on a peaceful afternoon, with only a few birds calling in the distance, but no other sound at all. Yet somehow his heart had beaten faster at the same time.

Then something utterly strange had happened. Suddenly Freddy had found he was looking at entirely different paintings, right where the other ones were before! These were also very good, but not as good as the ones he'd just seen. Also, he could more readily make out people in some, trees or mountains in others, and so on. Then it had come to Freddy that he'd been looking forward in time... to what this painter *would* do. He'd looked again. Yes, he could see from the paintings in front of him how this might come about. There was a word for what he'd seen before – what was it again? Yes, a *premonition* – it was seeing what would happen before it happened. 'This is all very weird', Freddy had thought.

It had been then that Ian appeared.... Freddy remembered it all very clearly and fondly. And what you've just read is exactly how Freddy did remember seeing Ian's paintings that first time.

Freddy and Ian never saw each other again. They both felt sad for a while about not being together, but they had strong and wonderful memories of each other – of their friendship – to help them in their lives. Ian's life had taken a different turn when he went to live on Bribie Island, and so had Freddy's when he moved in with Nicola and Tom.

Ian did think from time to time of making a trip to Darwin to see if he could find Freddy, especially after he heard from Maie about

Freddy's visit to her. But more than it being a long way, he had no idea of where in Darwin Freddy might be – he might not even have returned to Darwin, for that matter. Freddy also realised he didn't have any idea – any idea *at all* – where Ian was. Freddy had no way of writing to Maie about this – even if Freddy had found something small enough for him to write with, an antechinus' handwriting is too small for anyone to read or even recognise as a message or an address. Freddy would not have been able to go to a post office, anyway: he'd have to wait in a queue, find a way to climb up on the counter, and then ask for a stamp in front of all the other customers. And how would he pay for the stamp? Freddy began to feel dizzy. He shook his head: it wouldn't work. There were only certain things an antechinus – even an antechinus like Freddy – could do.

Freddy could have asked Nicola and Tom to help him. He did think about doing so. But no, Freddy preferred his life the way it was with them. Also, to suddenly speak after having been silent for so long would be too much of a shock for them both, he felt sure.

But Freddy never forgot Ian. Nor did Ian ever forget Freddy. How could they have, after all? They had been the best of friends, and they had crossed the Timor Sea together on a raft.

JAY AND THE FLAMINGO

J ay, who was in her early thirties, was an artist. She had been working on a painting that afternoon, but it had not been going well, or at least, as well as she'd hoped. She'd already been working on it for some time now, and it had come to be the only painting she was involved with. Her husband Wally was painting in his own studio in the house, so Jay went by herself to a nearby park – a large park with a zoo in it.

Jay walked around the park until she came to the zoo, then she walked around the enclosures until she stood in front of where the larger birds lived. There were no other people about, and it felt peaceful to be there. Jay leaned against a tree and took out her cigarettes.

'That's very bad for your health, dear', someone said.

Jay looked around her, but this part of the zoo still seemed deserted. 'I must be imagining things', thought Jay.

'However, I know it's really none of my business', the same someone said.

'Who said that? Where are you?' called out Jay.

'I'm right here.'

The only creature at all close to Jay was a pink flamingo. It had been edging its way closer for some time now, but Jay had thought nothing of it.

'Are you… are you able to speak?' Jay asked, as surprised with herself as she was with the idea of a talking flamingo.

'Yes, dear, I am', replied the flamingo, coming even closer. 'My name is Beatrice. And what is yours, if I may ask?'

'It's Jay.'

'Ah, what a nice name, my dear! And what do you do, if you don't mind my asking?'

'I'm an artist, but my painting isn't going very well, I'm afraid.'

'Why don't you paint a rose, my dear?'

'Beatrice, that's uncanny – I *am* painting a rose! Well, in a way... it's a rose and it's also not a rose.' And Jay struggled to explain this to Beatrice, while the flamingo listened attentively. When Jay had finished, Beatrice asked:

'What else do you do, Jay?'

'I love to dance, for one thing.'

'Well, I don't dance, dear, but I like to *move about*', replied Beatrice.

Jay promised to visit her again, and then left.

....

On the way home, Jay took a route that led past a hair salon which she was curious about. She knew the owner slightly, and she knew that he'd been intending to staff the salon with apes and monkeys borrowed from the zoo – gorillas, baboons and orang-utans, all known for their love of grooming. He felt they could be trained to be hair stylists. It would be a fashionable novelty, he thought, and it might make his fortune.

When Jay reached the salon, she peered in and indeed saw an orang-utan using its fingers to style a woman's hair. The woman seemed to be highly pleased with the way her hair was being stroked into place (presumably after being searched for insects). The owner, Bill, noticed Jay and waved. Jay waved back, but she didn't go in.

......

When Jay arrived back at her apartment, she told Wally about her encounter with Beatrice.

Wally didn't believe what she said about the flamingo. 'Jay, you've been working too hard!' he exclaimed. Jay didn't know how to persuade him.

Later, in the evening, their friend Wallace came by the apartment. Wallace was also an artist, and he published an unusual magazine with loose cards and pages in an envelope or small folder, with his own art and poetry and that of his friends and others. Jay told Wallace about Beatrice, and he was intrigued. He suggested that Jay, Wally and he go to the zoo together the next day.

....

'Beatrice, this is my husband Wally', Jay said.

'Hi, Beatrice', said Wally.

Beatrice didn't reply. She just looked at them in a steady kind of way.

'And I'm their friend Wallace. But some people call me Wally as well – so feel free.'

Beatrice remained silent.

'You know, I have a sister named Beatrice', said Wallace. Jay and Wally both looked at him, surprised; he'd never mentioned this before. Indeed, Wallace rarely said anything about his background.

Beatrice the flamingo didn't reply.

Jay, Wally and Wallace looked at each other. Wallace shrugged. Wally shook his head. Jay looked at Beatrice. Then Jay, Wally and Wallace turned and walked away.

......

The next time that Jay visited the zoo, Beatrice said to her: 'Are all the men you know called Wally, dear?'

'No, Beatrice, they're not', said Jay. 'And why didn't you speak to Wally and Wallace? I felt like a fool.'

'Oh, I'm sorry, my dear. You see, I'm a little... capricious like that. It wasn't anything personal: I'm sure Wally and Wallace are very nice.'

While they'd been talking, Jay had noticed two Canada geese moving closer and closer towards the flamingo.

Jay quickly climbed over the railings and jumped down into the enclosure.

'Oh dear, you *did* startle me!' exclaimed Beatrice.

'I just saved your life!' said Jay. 'Don't you realise that? I mean, if I hadn't been here...'

'Now, Jay, don't be so dramatic. I do appreciate your friendship, my dear, but *saving my life*! Let's not get carried away.'

Beatrice really could be utterly unaware of things, thought Jay. 'But there were two Canada geese – coming towards you! I'm sure they were going to attack you.'

'That must have been Guy and Anne. You didn't frighten them

away, did you? Jay, they're my good friends – they're the nicest, most *civilised* birds you could ever meet! Dear, dear me, now I'll have to go and apologise to them.'

'I can't seem to do anything right', thought Jay. 'Why on earth did I think Guy and Anne wanted to *attack* Beatrice?' She sighed.

'Goodbye, Beatrice', she said. 'I'll see you again soon.'

'See you soon, dear', said Beatrice.

......

On her way home, Jay looked in the window of the salon again.

An orang-utan, a gorilla and a baboon were grooming the hair of three stylish-looking women seated in front of mirrors. Other women sat waiting their turn. Bill was standing there, in a corner, and he noticed Jay and beckoned her in.

Bill introduced her briefly to Rosalind, the gorilla, Muriel, the baboon, and Annabelle, the orang-utan. Rosalind and Muriel stopped work just long enough to nod hello, but Jay could have sworn that Annabelle winked at her.

As she resumed walking towards her home, she wondered: Did they have long enough lunch breaks? And what happened to them in the evenings? Did they have a TV? And where did they sleep? Did they go back to the zoo?

....

Jay tried one more time to get Beatrice to talk to other people. She asked her poet friend Jack to accompany her when she next visited the flamingo.

Beatrice wasn't really familiar with people being drunk, but she could tell there was something wrong with Jack.

'Beatrice, this is Jack', said Jay.

Beatrice didn't say anything.

'So, you can't talk!' said Jack in a slurred voice, and he began laughing. 'Can't talk, can't talk!'

'Jack!' exclaimed Jay. 'That's not nice.'

'Of course I can talk!' said Beatrice.

Jack fainted. When he came to, he swore he'd never drink alcohol again. And he didn't – for a day or two.

....

Jay struggled with her painting for a long time. Some days her work on it went well, while other days felt discouraging. She persisted. The painting changed variously, and she could have made a series of related paintings instead, but she didn't. Why? The painting was extremely large and heavy, for one thing. There wasn't space in her studio for more than one work like it. However, there was also a sense of wanting one final image, not several.

She didn't visit the salon again, but she heard that Annabelle, Muriel and Rosalind had become celebrated hair stylists.

She did continue to visit Beatrice.

Finally, Jay took a photograph of the painting to show Beatrice. 'Beatrice, the painting is finished – or at least, as far as it can be', she said.

'Oh my dear, how wonderful!' Beatrice exclaimed.

Jay held the photograph for Beatrice to see.

It was and was not a rose. It wasn't red. For the most part it was grey and white. It was centred, like a rose, but it didn't really look like a rose in any conventional way. Yet it did somehow seem flower-like.

It was a painting, but the paint was so thick that it was almost a sculpture, as well. Parts of the encrusted surface seemed carved rather than painted.

There was something raw about it, yet sophisticated at the same time. It had the look of something long considered and meditated upon, but there were also hints of the impulsive and the energetic. Despite the grey and black, it wasn't dull in the slightest.

In fact, more than anything else it was like an extraordinary burst of light, along severe radiating lines, out of and back into what might be clouds and might also be plant forms. At the bottom of the painting these forms became more like mounds of earth or stones. It had an intensity to it which was like dazzling sunlight breaking through the boughs and leaves of trees or the gaps in a wall.

Guy and Anne had been edging nearer and nearer, until they looked at the photograph over Beatrice's folded wings. 'Splendour!' said Guy. 'Brilliance!' said Anne. Jay was taken back: she had never realised that they too could talk; but she didn't say anything.

'Dear, dear Jay', said Beatrice, 'it's beautiful! Not pretty, mind you, not at all. Indeed, I think this is even more than just beautiful – it's magnificent.'

Guy and Anne nodded approvingly.

'Do you really think so, Beatrice?' Jay asked.

'My dear, a flamingo always tells the truth. Didn't you know?'

HOW BERT THE HOOPOE WENT TO ISRAEL
AND WHAT HAPPENED THERE

Bert always sensed that he was different. He became more aware of this as time passed, even though his parents attempted – for some while, at least – to make light of it. Sometimes they even lied to him, for what they thought was his own good… or perhaps their own. This wasn't the best thing to do, however.

'Why do I have feathers when you don't?' asked Bert one day.

'We do have some, underneath our clothes. The others we decided to pluck.'

'Should I pluck mine?'

'No, no, yours are beautiful! Your crest feathers especially….'

'Did you have crests, too?'

'Yes, but ours fell out.'

'Will mine?'

'Oh, no, dear! Not yours.'

'Why?'

'Well, yours are… *better* than ours were.'

Bert's singing voice was also different. He had a fine voice, but he could really sing only two different notes. However, he sang them well and also enthusiastically. In contrast, his parents both sang many notes, but rather poorly. Bert, they would say, was a *minimalist* without knowing it – he could achieve much with very little, just as a painter might make a wonderful painting with just a few simple lines and colours.

Things only became worse when Bert, who had been schooled at home in his village in Shropshire, went to Oxford University. He had seldom had any contact with children or adolescents; now he found himself surrounded by young people. For the most part the other students didn't shun him, and some were friendly, but he often felt he was the object of curiosity. This was true with the lecturers, as well. Why? Because as Bert had always thought, he was *different*.

Then one day something highly significant happened. Bert was studying English literature (and also writing poetry), and one of his student friends, Julia, was also studying English literature while in her spare time she studied bird life, or ornithology, if you prefer. (And she was writing poetry, too.) On this particular day, when they were at lunch, Julia said, 'Isn't it very *unusual* for a hoopoe to be able to talk?'

'For a *what*?' exclaimed Bert, indignantly. 'I'm a human! I have human parents.'

'Bert', said Julia patiently, 'please have a look in this book I'm reading. Here's an illustration of a hoopoe. Doesn't it look like you?'

Bert looked at the picture, and what Julia said was true enough.

'Isn't it difficult writing with a pen in your beak?' asked Julia.

'My *what*? Don't you mean my *mouth*?'

'No, Bert, come on, now. It's a beak. But I can see that you wouldn't be able to handle a pen with your wings. And while we're on the subject… doesn't it sometimes feel awkward being so much… *smaller* than the rest of us at uni?'

'You said the "s"-word!' said Bert. 'That word wasn't allowed at home!'

'Bert, you must have realized that you're really a bird, even if a most unusually gifted one.'

34

It was as if the paving stones had broken apart under his feet… but it was also as if a semi-dark room had suddenly been flooded by light. He'd read about such experiences, and that was indeed how they were described.

'My parents!' said Bert, who was still struggling with the truth. 'They look like you do.'

'They must have *adopted* you', replied Julia.

That weekend, Bert was sitting at dinner with his parents; he speared the last morsel on his plate with his beak and ate it, and then he took a deep breath and repeated what Julia had said.

'Oh dear', said Mabel, Bert's adoptive mother. 'I guess we always knew you'd find out one day, but we hoped against hope that you wouldn't! Yes, we did adopt you, dear.'

'And we taught you to talk and to read and write', said Peter, Bert's adoptive father. 'And brought you up to be a fine person…um, bird.'

'We wanted you to be the son we never had and never could have', said Mabel, who was beginning to cry.

'Don't be upset', said Bert. 'I just wish you'd told me.'

'Somehow we couldn't bring ourselves to tell you that you weren't our real son', said Mabel, before she dabbed at her eyes and then blew her nose.

'I understand', said Bert, although he wasn't completely sure that he did.

……..

After Bert graduated, he took a job teaching students to write poetry, at a university in... but does it matter *where*? It might have been in the Midlands or it might have been in Bedfordshire... or practically anywhere in England. He soon found that teaching in a university was not a suitable job for a poet or a hoopoe, or for that matter a human being. Too many hours, too many student papers to mark, too much red tape, too much paperwork, too many meetings, too many pointless tasks imposed by the people at the top: it all began to wear him down. He wondered how his own lecturers had coped, but as time went on he heard that many of them had quit, taken early retirement, or... died. Bert didn't want to die because of stress. He felt that his crest feathers were wilting. He wanted to be someplace where his poetry would be taken seriously, and he wouldn't need to teach.

Then one day he received an e-mail from his old friend and fellow student Julia. Amongst other things, including news of her researches into bird life, she wrote: "By the way, did you know that the hoopoe is the national bird of Israel?"

This was what he had been waiting for. Israel! *That* was where hoopoes were truly appreciated. Surely if he went there his poetry would be acclaimed, and he would become famous. He'd never need to teach again.

(Bert had yet to learn that if you want to make a reasonable living, poetry is not your best bet, or even a good bet, no matter where you are. In fact, for the most part it's not even a bet at all.)

Bert quit his job, said goodbye for the time being to Peter and Mabel, and bought a plane ticket for Israel. Fortunately he'd been taught several languages by his adoptive parents, including Hebrew, so he felt well prepared.

....

Bert had been in Jerusalem for three weeks, and things had not gone as he'd expected.

Although there were no other hoopoes who wrote poetry, at least as far as he could find out, there were plenty of hoopoes in Israel and plenty of poets. 'Upstart! What a nerve!' he heard one poet exclaim when Bert introduced himself at a reading as "the National Poetry Bird".

It was all rather discouraging. There were no offers of publication, no invitations to large readings. He might have decided to go home right there and then… except that something unforeseen occurred.

Bert was taking a stroll one afternoon, thinking about what he should do, when a car pulled up suddenly and someone pulled him inside and drove off. Besides the driver, there were three other men in the car; the one nearest slipped a blindfold over Bert's eyes. 'Shut up or we will pull your crest feathers out!' he shouted in English.

Bert did as he was told. Or rather, he fainted.

……..

He came to in complete darkness. He could hear men talking quietly in Arabic, which he could also understand. Peter and Mabel had achieved much with his home schooling.

Then he realised that he was still blindfolded.

'Could you take the blindfold off, please?' he called out.

'Ah, you speak Arabic! In a minute, National Poetry Bird!' someone said gruffly. 'We are just getting ready to film you.'

And indeed he was filmed, sitting under a bright light while his captors gathered around him, wearing masks and holding guns.

They identified themselves as a group of Palestinian freedom fighters. (Bert was still somewhat dazed and didn't take in the group's name.) They referred to him as the National Poetry Bird of Israel, and clearly thought the Israelis would release some of their comrades who were being held prisoner as long as Bert remained unharmed and eventually released. Otherwise, they said, they would kill him. And with that they turned the camera off. Bert was in a state of utter disbelief. He felt like he might pass out again, but managed to get a grip on himself.

'The Israelis will never do what you're demanding!' he said after a few deep breaths.

'Of course they will!' one of the men said. 'You're the National Poetry Bird, after all.'

'But that's just something I call myself. And how on earth did you hear about it? I only announced it at a single poetry reading.'

'Ah, National Poetry Bird, word gets around, believe me. You don't think we have ears with which to hear?' the same man replied.

'You're completely mistaken!' Bert said. 'No one is going to release your comrades because of a hoopoe who writes poetry.'

'Shut up, National Poetry Bird. Who asked you what you thought about this?' The others nodded in agreement.

Bert suddenly became angry. He puffed himself up, and his crest stiffened and then began to quiver with rage. 'Do you know what I'm going to do? I'm going to write an epic poem mocking you and your friends! Everyone will laugh at you when I'm finished. It will go on for page after page after page after page after page....'

Ten minutes later Bert stopped saying "after page". It seemed long enough for an epic poem, especially when he didn't really have much at all to say.

Strangely, no one had even tried to interrupt him. They all looked taken aback. Finally, the man who had speaking with Bert locked eyes with him, and then began to smile.

'For the National Poetry Bird of Israel, you have guts! I think I like you!'

The other men followed his lead, to Bert's amazement, and they were soon playing cards with him, as well as singing songs together. Bert's impressive voice was much appreciated, even if he could only sing two notes.

'What is your name, National Poetry Bird?' asked the man who did most of the talking and was clearly the spokesman. 'Or are you just called National Poetry Bird?'

'My name is Bert.'

'Do you have a last name as well?'

'Bert.'

'Your name is Bert Bert?' the man asked, raising an eyebrow.

'No, it's just Bert. I only have the one name.'

'That's very sad, National Poetry Bird, to only have the one name. I myself have more than one, but I cannot tell you what they are. You understand.'

'It's not sad', said Bert. 'It's just how it is. Well, I did have a last name, but when I found out I'd been adopted I decided to just call myself Bert. The people who adopted me don't seem to mind that I don't use their last name.'

After a minute or so, Bert asked: 'What is your group called? I didn't quite catch it.'

'We're called the P. Oulipo.'

'You're called *what?*'

'We used to be called the Palestinian Oulipo, but we decided to shorten it to P. Oulipo. We were an experimental writing group –'

'You were *what?*'

'Please stop saying "*what?*", Bert. We then became politicised, but kept the name. After a while we were fed up with just writings things – manifestoes, essays, poems, songs, however political – and decided to *act*. Now we kidnap people, blow up cars and buildings…. We make a difference.'

'And you still kept the name?'

'Why not? It's our identity.'

'So let me get this straight: you've gone from being literary extremists to being political extremists?'

'We would not put it that way, Bert. We've gone from being *literary experimentalists* to being *freedom fighters*.'

Clearly *my* freedom isn't an issue, thought Bert.

A couple of days went by and nothing happened about arrangements for Bert's release. Conversations took place in hushed voices amongst his captors.

Finally the spokesman for the group said: 'Look, Bert, our demands have not been met. But we've decided to make a very big exception and let you escape. It's either that or we kill you, and for once we'd rather not do that.'

'You mean you're letting me go?'

'No, we couldn't do that. We're letting you escape instead.'

'Thank you', said Bert. 'It's not like I *approve* of you – I mean, you kidnap people, you kill people, sometimes you kidnap *and* kill people. And it's not as if all Palestinians approve of the sort of things you do, either. But we've been getting on really well, in spite of everything. And of course I appreciate it that you're letting me escape.'

'Bert! What about how the Israelis have treated *us*? And we were here long before these upstarts. The State of Israel! Bah! And don't you think there are Israeli terrorists?'

Bert thought it best not to argue. People who believe in Causes (with a capital "C") are not always amenable to dialogue. 'How am I going to escape?' he asked.

'Perhaps you could say you overpowered us and then ran off.'

'I'm not sure that would sound very impressive for you. After all, a small bird overpowering four men….'

'OK, perhaps we made the mistake of leaving just one man to guard you. I mean, we really do that sometimes.'

'It still doesn't sound very impressive for you….'

'Look, Bert, perhaps we can't let you escape after all?'

'No, no, no! What about if I say I found some sleeping pills and put them in your drinks when you weren't looking? And then when you were all asleep, I escaped.'

The spokesman nodded and smiled. 'It makes you sound sneaky! I like it!'

The P. Oulipo were wishing Bert goodbye, when suddenly the front door came crashing down, and a large, strange-looking figure appeared in the doorway. The terrorists grabbed their weapons and opened fire, but it seemed to have no effect.

'LET HIM GO!!!' the strange creature, who looked like a man and yet not like a man, roared.

Most of the group made for the back door. Their spokesman, however, held his ground. 'Who are you? *What* are you?' he asked in a trembling voice.

'I AM THE GOLEM!!!' the Golem roared. 'LET THAT BIRD GO!!!' And without waiting for a reply, he advanced into the room and put out his hands to grab the Palestinian.

'You stop right there!' Bert yelled.

The Golem stopped and looked back at Bert. 'WHAT???!!!' he roared.

'Could you stop shouting as if you were doing it in capital letters and with several exclamation marks?'

'Well, all right. If you say so! But I'm rescuing you; and this… *this* is the bad guy. I'll rip him to shreds!'

'You don't understand…. OK, he kidnaps and kills people, but he's been nice to me since he kidnapped me! Oh, I don't know, it's all so complicated – but please don't harm him!'

'Thank you, Bert! I will never forget you', said the P. Oulipoist, who rushed past the bemused Golem and out the door.

'Who are you again?' Bert asked the Golem, who was still recovering his composure.

'I'm the Golem. I was made of clay by a great Rabbi in Prague, many centuries ago. He placed a scroll of the Holy Scripture in my chest to bring me to life. I was created to help Jews who were being persecuted. By the way, you can call me Frank.'

'Isn't that a slightly odd name for a Golem?'

'*I* like it. I chose it myself. And I'm *the* Golem, not *a* Golem.'

'Sorry', replied Bert. 'But how do you come to be in Israel?'

'I emigrated. After all, I'm a good Jew. I belong here. Whereas those Palestinians…. Upstarts! We Jews simply reclaimed our land, that's all.'

Again, Bert didn't want to enter into a discussion about the Israeli-Palestinian situation. But he asked: 'Surely there are many good Jews who haven't emigrated here?'

'Well, I can't speak for everyone….' he said. 'Listen, have you eaten, by any chance? If not, I know a place that does a mean falafel and hummus with pita.'

'Let's go', said Bert, who was famished.

'By the way, when I said "mean", that was slang. In other words, it's *really good*.'

'I think I got that', said Bert.

Both on the way to the restaurant and after they'd sat down at a table, the huge Golem not surprisingly attracted a great deal of attention. But more surprisingly, so did Bert. There were recurrent whispers of 'It's the National Poetry Bird!' and 'Look, the National Poetry Bird is free!' and the like.

'Yes', said Frank, without being asked, 'you're a celebrity. That film of you has been shown on TV, and you were identified by those terrorists as the National Poetry Bird. Most of us didn't even know we had a National Poetry Bird. But then some people came forward who had heard you read your poems, and they were interviewed on TV and in the papers. The most surprising thing we found out is that you're not an Israeli, even though you are a hoopoe, our national bird. So no one quite knew who should take responsibility for you. Israelis said that although you're the National Poetry Bird, the English should somehow arrange for your release. The English said that they couldn't do anything about the terrorists' demands, and besides, you're Israel's National Poetry Bird, even if you do come from England. It was a stalemate. So I decided to take things into my own hands. Someone had to.'

'Thank you, Frank. Um… I've been meaning to say something about this before, but did you know you have several bullet holes in you?'

'Oh, don't worry about that! It doesn't hurt. I'm made of clay, remember. And I can patch up the holes anytime I feel like it.' Frank looked at his watch. 'Ah, I must run! Busy, busy, busy! Catch you later.' So saying, he put down some money for the meal and left.

Bert noticed that Frank had left enough money for both of their meals. 'What an interesting guy… um, creature', said Bert to himself.

……..

Bert found himself the object of considerable attention. He was interviewed several times, and while in no way condoning his captors, he said that he'd not been mistreated, and that he ended up getting on with them. Not all such groups would have behaved so well, he fully agreed, but the facts were the facts. (He omitted to mention the threat to his head feathers. And he only referred to Frank as a stranger who had unexpectedly aided him. The story sounded strange enough

as it was, especially as Bert refused to go into details about either why
the group came to respect him or how exactly he managed to escape.
He kept silent about these things, which many believed to be because
he was still somewhat in a state of shock over his ordeal. He always
displayed a dignity worthy of... well, someone who plays the mando-
lin in church, for instance.)

He became famous... and controversial. Some praised what they saw
as his bravery, and speculated on his ingenuity in escaping. Others
doubted his story, and in some cases claimed that he was insulting
victims of freedom fighters... or extremists... or terrorists by saying
he'd been "treated well". (Bert sympathised, but stuck to his story.)
Many would have preferred him to openly take sides; while some
praised his independent and balanced attitude.

As a result of his fame, Bert became widely published and reviewed,
and he gave many readings. He expected to be asked to read at Poetry
International, a large literary festival back in England, but the invitation never came. Not only this: even in Israel invitations to publish
and read his poetry eventually stopped. That's when Bert realised
something important: as it's often been said, fame is fickle. People forgot about who he was, and unless he was kidnapped again, it didn't
seem that they would ever return to thinking about him in the way
they had.

Discouraging as this was, something happened to brighten his mood.
He received an invitation to read in a poetry series in London called
The Cool Black Caravan. This wasn't exactly Poetry International,
in fact it was a small monthly event attended by a modest number of
people. Yet Bert knew it by reputation, and knew that only the most
adventurous, probing and talented poets were asked to take part. Not
having any plans to cancel in Israel, he took the first flight he could
find back to England.

So Bert found his real audience as a poet. He was no longer read or
listened to because he was the National Poetry Bird, who had escaped

from the P. Oulipo and become a famous yet controversial figure. Now his poetry was admired for its own sake, even if by far fewer people.

Something else happened, at least as important, or so Bert thought. At his reading at The Cool Black Caravan, Bert had noticed a bat hanging from the chandelier. He didn't think too much about this, as nothing really seemed strange to him anymore. Nor did he find it all that strange when it turned out that he could understand what the bat said and she could understand him

'Hello', said the bat. 'I really like your poetry, especially the darker bits of it.'

'Thank you', said Bert. 'Do you write poetry? And what's your name, if I may ask?'

'I'm Leonora. I do compose poetry from time to time, but I mainly write horror fiction. Oh, and in case you're wondering, I read my work into a special recording device. It's such a great invention for a bat!'

They were soon chatting away and making plans to meet again. In time, they became close companions.

Bert would later say, in fact, that this was the best thing to come out of his visit to Israel, his subsequent brief fame and his return to England. As hoopoes go, Bert was a romantic… or a sentimentalist, some would say. He'd prefer "romantic".

And so would I, the author of this story.

(In memory of Mathias Goeritz)

THE MIRROR OF THE FATAL SHORE

"I wept and wailed when I saw the unfamiliar land...."
(Empedocles)

1.

The English authorities began to send convicts to Australia on January 18, 1787; arriving at Botany Bay after a long voyage and then moving on to Port Jackson (now Sydney Harbour), where they landed on January 26 of the following year. This formed the earliest of many penal colonies in Australia, with transportations to Van Diemen's Land (Tasmania), Victoria, Queensland and Western Australia following on from those first to New South Wales. This penal system lasted for several decades, with the last transportation – to Western Australia – occurring in 1868.

It was entirely possible to be sent to Australia as a convict for trifling offences –misdemeanours, really – as well as for graver crimes: those who had acted from sheer desperate need and stolen this or that to stave off starvation were transported alongside vicious wrongdoers and those who had carried on a career of criminal behaviour. Many died either during the voyage or soon after landing, such were the conditions on the transportation ships. How they were treated in the unfamiliar land varied, without a doubt, depending largely upon those in charge in a particular area and at a particular time, and so forth; however, the worst of the settlements – at Norfolk Island, for instance, or Moreton Bay – became notorious for the inhumanity, the brutality that thrived there, forcing the convicts to lead a spirit-numbing existence.

This is all, of course, well known.

What isn't, for few people knew it then, nor indeed know it now, is that a similar penal colony was set up in the early 1800s – accounts differ as to the date – at Herne Bay in England, consisting of prisoners sent over from Australia.

The prisoners in question were koalas.

2.

Eucalyptus trees were unknown to the English before they came to Australia; but it was as early as 1788 that surgeons on that First Fleet transporting convicts, discovered the medicinal qualities of the oil derived from the leaves of this tree.

It was found that eucalyptus oil could be used to treat colds, bronchitis and influenza; and that it was also useful as an antiseptic for wounds and as a precaution against infection. Later on the oil proved to have other possibilities, depending on the quantity employed and what it was combined with: as an insect repellent; in fragrances; even as a flavouring.

Long before the commercial distilling and sale of eucalyptus oil was successfully started in 1852, in Victoria, a wildly unsuccessful attempt occurred in England, sometime in the early 1800s.

It happened this way:

An extremely erratic and eccentric businessman, who had succeeded in some commercial endeavours, due to luck, but mostly failed, came up with the notion of bringing koalas, whose diet consists exclusively of eucalyptus leaves, to England, together with eucalyptus trees in tubs. There the captive koalas would be forced to extract the oil from the leaves, and this would be refined and then bottled and sold.

Extraordinarily, he found backers, one of whom had recently purchased land at Herne Bay and was willing to give this over as a place for the koalas and for the refining and bottling procedures. This would appear to have been decisive in transporting the koalas, following on from the erratic businessman's curious obsession with the idea; and although basing the operation in Australia would have been far simpler in some regards, it would have required successive voyages to deliver the bottled eucalyptus oil, as the market was mainly back in England.

What *were* they thinking of? They weren't really thinking at all. They wanted to make money, and this blinded them.

The businessman who came up with the idea was in fact a little mad. And like certain others who are somewhat crazy, yet not quite certifiable by doctors to be kept in an asylum, he could be charming and oddly persuasive: charismatic, in fact. When he started talking, people stopped thinking, and it could take quite some time for them to begin thinking again. (In this he was rather like those political leaders, crazed or at least half-crazed with power, who incite needless wars; although in their case the people who have been led astray by them sometimes never start thinking again.) It took time; but eventually the sheer inadequacies of his plans became evident.

'Who better to extract eucalyptus oil than koalas? They *live off* eucalyptus leaves! And we don't have to pay them – they're just these little animals! What's more, we'll have them *arrested* first!'

Needless to say, the plan was impracticable. Trying to force koalas to spit out the masticated remains of their leaves, so that liquid could then be separated from pulp, and use this as the basis for commercial eucalyptus oil, was folly indeed. Yet so greedy and so deluded were the man's backers, and in a few cases so influential, that koalas in New South Wales were rounded up and deported to Herne Bay to work as convict labour.

This was how it was accomplished: the koalas to be deported from Australia were described as "marsupial miscreants" (and sometimes as "miscreant marsupials"). However, the koalas were in fact picked at random, not selected on the basis of any supposedly vicious or "unlawful" behaviour. And it's hard to see on what basis any such selection *could* have been made. It appears that these small, inoffensive creatures were somehow, inexplicably, arbitrarily, considered to be "miscreant" by nature or in essence.

....

Now, koalas, though sometimes referred to as *bears,* are not bears at all; they are indeed marsupials, creatures that carry their young in pouches; and therefore bearing a relation to wombats and, more distantly, kangaroos and wallabies. They are small enough to be quite easily cradled by a human, and look endearingly stumpy and stout; they're covered by fur – grey or brown for the most part, with white fur extending from beneath the nose and around the mouth then down the chin and neck and right down their entire front, and luxuriant white and grey or brown fluffy fur on the large ears on their large, round heads, which also sport a large black nose. A black nose in a grey face might possibly sound odd; but in fact koalas have pleasant and amiable-looking faces – quite handsome, if not perhaps pretty, in fact.

While they do engage in squabbles over territory – trees, in particular – and mating partners, for the most part they lead quiet lives, aided by the naturally intoxicating effects of their diet and a great deal of sleep in any given day. And if they fall out of their trees, their skulls contain a cushioning fluid surrounding the brain. Their main enemies are human predators, whether they kill for food, as with the Aborigines, or even just for sport, as with some whites. The other main danger to their lives is bushfires, for eucalyptus trees are highly flammable.

Koalas are usually solitary creatures, except for mating and – in the case of the adult females – the rearing of their young. But in a forest somewhere in New South Wales, there once lived a large number of koalas who were far more social in their ways.

They were different for one reason only.

They had Norman.

Norman was their Koala Elder. No one seemed to know where he'd come from, but he'd arrived one day in their midst and began to teach, in any way he could: by example, by physical and vocal signs, and so forth. Amongst other things, he taught that it was preferable to live in harmony with each other, to share and to help. He also encouraged closer and more faithful relations between mating partners. Gradually he found converts; and eventually they were all converted.

One other thing needs to be said about this strange koala named Norman. He could understand English and taught it to the others, while swearing them to silence about this acquisition. It was a secret asset and a source of strength.

......

David, who if you like is the hero of our story, was amongst the first of the koalas to be captured for deportation. He was part of the company of koalas who followed Norman's teachings.

Peaceful by natural inclination as well as belief, David had to occasionally deal with wandering males – young male koalas not affiliated with any group – who would make unwanted attentions to his partner, Doreen. He didn't enjoy fights – hated them in fact – and would try to warn the koalas off by bellowing, but sometimes this didn't work and he was forced to use his claws and his teeth.

On the fateful day in question, he'd been asleep, which was not surprising: koalas sleep for between eighteen and twenty hours a day. Doreen was curled up beside him. They were awakened by a ruckus: human shouts and curses, and sleepy koala growls followed by screams and bellowing. Koalas were being knocked down from their trees with poles, and caught in nets or forced into burlap bags. Some clambered to safety, some managed to claw their way free of the nets and run away, but others were not so fortunate.

David and Doreen were knocked to the ground and found themselves cornered.

'Let's have some fun!' one of the men shouted, advancing on Doreen as if to hit her with a club.

Doreen immediately looked at David beseechingly. David rushed at the man and scratched his leg with his powerful claws. The man yelped with pain, and then kicked David in the stomach. David groaned in agony and rolled over, tears flowing down his furry cheeks.

The man stood over him, forgetting for the moment about Doreen. She hesitated at first, looking over towards where David lay. Then, understanding what he'd done, she nodded, and scampered away into the bush.

They were never to see each other again.

David was sick for at least a week, during which time he was forced into the hold of a ship bound for England, amongst many other koalas. The others – or at least, those who were also Norman's followers – did what they could to help him. (He was well liked by his fellows, for one thing.)

Whatever else, he'd distracted attention from his beloved Doreen, allowing her to escape. That was all he'd hoped to achieve.

'Great Spirit Koala!' he prayed, 'please let her remain safe. May she find a good mate in place of me, and be happy!'

......

I don't wish to dwell on the miseries of these small creatures, torn from their land, in many cases torn from family and separated from friends. I must touch on them, however. Koalas are used to freedom of movement, in trees and on the ground; they live their lives in the fresh air, in sunlight and natural darkness. They need large quantities of eucalyptus leaves, relative to their size, as their only source of nutrition; and despite what is sometimes said and written about them – namely, that they don't actually drink – they need some water, the males (who are larger) more than the females.

The voyage to England took around six months, with the ship travelling through the Bass Strait and then making only brief stops, to take on food rations and rum for the sailors, and barrels of water – most of which was for the eucalyptus trees. These trees were in huge tubs, lashed to the deck and masts. The decks had been specially reinforced to support the unaccustomed load; and in order that the trees didn't slow the ship, sails were rigged from the trunks. Unusually strong winds favoured their passage.

During the voyage, the koalas were kept in a partitioned space within a dark, almost airless hold; crowded together so that precious little movement was possible. Although the ship carried sacks of eucalyptus leaves for more immediate use, the koalas didn't at first even recognise the plucked leaves as food, so habituated were they to eating straight from branches. After that, the sailors grudgingly and sparingly fed the koalas with leaves from the trees. Little water came their way, either.

Many koalas died, of course. Those who survived were malnourished and dehydrated, and ended up sleeping even more than usual. Much weakened, with limbs that ached from being in the confined space, they were dispirited and disoriented.

Most of them had tried their best to share their rations, however inadequate; there was no sense of *territory* here, and besides, many had been instilled with Norman's views on sharing and mutuality. Some koalas, however, had ended up resorting to violence to claim food and water; but those who did were pounced upon by the others and lost whatever they'd momentarily gained: they soon desisted.

When the prisoners arrived at Deptford, the living were separated from the dead, and the dead burned on a large fire. The survivors, though in such a sorry state they could barely move, were herded onto another ship, bound for Herne Bay. (For some reason, the trees were dispatched on a different ship, after a quantity of leaves had been taken on board the koalas' vessel.) This time they were kept in cages on the deck, and owing to the deaths of so many they were not as crowded as before. There must also have been some kinder sailors on this ship, because they were fed and watered more generously during the short voyage.

....

David was amongst the koalas who survived that terrible journey from Port Jackson to Deptford, and the subsequent journey to Herne Bay.

He had not been one of those koalas who in order to have more food and water for themselves tried to keep it from the mouths of others. It was simply not how he was; besides, he didn't believe the Great Spirit Koala would want him to behave that way.

Like all the rest of the survivors, he was weak and exhausted when he arrived at the compound at Herne Bay; the more generous rations on board the ship from Deptford had not helped greatly in restoring him, given how brief a journey it had been. He was also heartbroken: he missed Doreen terribly.

For the most part, the people in charge of the compound were not at all kind; however, they realised that the koalas needed, at the very least, to be kept alive. Too many had perished already. They had a diminished work force on their hands; and a fresh supply of convict koalas would take quite some time coming from Australia.

So, the koalas were allowed adequate food and water, although only *just*, and allowed to move freely within their wire enclosure. To prevent them from eating what was considered too much, the guards stood on ladders and prodded them away from their leaves from time to time with poles, and sometimes even knocked them out of the branches. The more sadistic of the guards would also do this for "fun".

The problem these captors now faced was how exactly they would put their prisoners to work.

......

The eccentric, or if you like, slightly mad businessman had by now decamped with various monies he'd collected from his investors. I would hazard a guess he wasn't crazy enough *not* to have done so.

The investors selected a foreman for the works.

The foreman was at a loss to know what to do.

The investors were also at a loss, but didn't want to admit it.

They supplied a quantity of pure eucalyptus oil that had been steam distilled at some cost. '*This* is what we need', they said. 'Make those little bastards *produce* it.'

Easier said than done, needless to say....

......

While these deliberations were going on, someone turned up at the compound bearing a sketchpad and a supply of pencils and pens and ink bottles. He began to sketch the koalas.

David snuck a look.

'What on earth is he doing?' whispered David.

'He's making a likeness, mate. It's called "art". He's what's known as an artist', one of the other koalas whispered back.

This koala wasn't from amongst Norman's followers, so David was surprised to find he knew English, but he was too polite to say anything.

Another man suddenly appeared and sidled up to the artist. 'Oh! I'm honoured! How did you ever find me?' exclaimed the artist.

The other man only smiled sagely, and began to look through the sketches.

'Ah, you've caught their inner spirit! Their *very being* is displayed in these sketches. Bravo! Bravo!'

The artist made a little bow. 'Your kindness is even more surpassing than your sagacity and acumen', he said.

'Do you think I could look at one of the little beggars at close quarters? Possibly *hold* it, even?' the other man asked.

One of the guards obligingly opened the gate to the enclosure, and the man reached in to grab hold of a koala.

It pissed on him. (After all, it didn't know what he intended.)

'Irritable little furry bugger!'

The gate was quickly closed again, and the man went off, shaking his head and wiping his hand with a scented handkerchief. Koala urine has a strong smell of eucalyptus about it. You definitely know when you've been urinated on by a koala.

'Who on earth was that?' David asked in a whisper.

'Apparently he's an art critic, mate.'

'An artist? Like the other man?'

'No, mate, he writes about art.'

'He does *what?*'

'Yeah, exactly, mate, exactly.'

David wondered how the other koala knew all this, but again he was too polite to ask.

....

David found he could entertain his captors by attempting headstands and handstands, and also by musical growling. He always fell over when he tried standing on his head or on his front paws, but his audience seemed to find this hilarious. Koalas can't exactly *sing*, but David adapted his natural growling sounds (often emitted as part of the act of bellowing) to semi-adequate approximations of songs he'd heard the guards singing. For the English he sang 'Shallow Brown' or 'Greensleeves', for the Irish he rendered 'My Love Nell' or the 'Londonderry Air'. He even varied his native bellowing so that it sounded like yodelling: this went down a treat. As a reward, they left off knocking him away from the eucalyptus leaves, unlike the other koalas, and also gave him extra water.

At first his companions thought David was being a toady and jeered at him. But when he quite clearly performed his antics to distract the guards from interfering with the others' feeding, as often as he could, they changed their minds. Gradually, they also realised he had a *purpose*: he was gathering his strength, with a view to escaping the compound and finding his way to freedom.

He never *spoke* to, or in front of, the guards, of course. They could never be allowed to know that koalas are capable of understanding and even speaking a human language (in however an odd growly way).

......

Frustrations grew, both amongst the financial backers of the scheme, because they could obtain no tangible results, and because they more and more suspected they'd been misled, if not downright swindled; and amongst the guards, who were also expected to be workmen, but who couldn't fathom what exactly else they were supposed to do than guard the koalas.

Yes, the aim was to use the koalas to extract eucalyptus oil from gum leaves.

But *how*?

How indeed do you make a koala spit out the chewed-up remains of the eucalyptus leaves they're eating? Even if you restrain the koala so that he or she doesn't claw you, they can still bite you... as well as piss on you. Gloves proved of limited use, especially as they made it difficult to prise open the creature's jaws... and the wearer still suffered splashing (the koala simply aimed differently).

(The impracticality of using the masticated remains spat out by a koala as the basis for commercial eucalyptus oil was something that still hadn't dawned on anyone at this point... though it would.)

There were even plans to rip out the koalas' claws and teeth, openly expressed in front of the creatures. This was revised to ripping out the claws and leaving the teeth, as a toothless koala can't be expected to *chew*. The plan was then abandoned, as clearly this was of no more use than restraining the creatures. Before this was realised, however, an attempt was made, and foiled.

When Norman, the Koala Elder, heard about what was intended, he cried in rage: 'Great Spirit Koala, may *their* nails be torn out, and *their* teeth, too!'

Norman also called the koalas to open resistance as a group if anything of the sort were attempted by the guards against any koala. The multiple clawing, biting and of course pissing that resulted when a solitary koala was grabbed with such an objective clearly in view (pliers had been produced) put pay to any enthusiasm on the part of the guards, however sadistic a few of them might be.

....

One day a man turned up at the compound, a man who the koalas had not seen there before.

David recognised him, however.

He recognised him from that fateful day back in Australia.

David couldn't help himself. When the man entered the enclosure, presumably with some purpose in mind, David saw red – literally, in as much as a red fog enveloped his sight, and within it he saw before him the man he hated: the man who had kicked him, captured him and exiled him – and separated him from his beloved Doreen. He flung himself at the man, clawing as hard and deep as he could. The man howled with pain.

A couple of the guards pulled David off his hated foe. This time David didn't wait to be kicked or hit with a club: he scampered away as fast as he could and prudently hid.

'You're a dead man!' the foe snarled. 'Um, koala', he then corrected himself. 'In fact, you're all dead! You're useless, all of you! We're selling you to some doctors who want to experiment on you – see how you like that! You'll die slow and excruciating deaths, and I'm glad!'

The koalas looked at one another. *Useless?* What on earth does *use* have to do with anything? (But of course that's all they ever were to these people – something to be made use of.)

None of them liked the sound of the phrase, "who want to experiment on you", though they weren't sure what it meant. "You'll all die slow and excruciating deaths" definitely didn't sound good.

The koalas all felt it was a bad day in Herne Bay.

....

David knew now that he had to escape, and that he had to do it *soon*.

He would have to scale the wire fence of the enclosure. This in itself was not too difficult, as koalas are experts at climbing, even if what they're used to climbing are trees.

The enclosure was always guarded by at least two men, day and night. They were armed with poles and clubs, and they could also call other guards to their aid if needed.

That was the real problem David faced.

From time to time, his captors had mentioned the undiluted eucalyptus oil, steam distilled from gum leaves. They had even said where it was stored. David fancied they would not like what it would do to them if they were tricked into drinking it. He thought he could cup the liquid in his paws and pour it into the whiskey they drank. Surely it would put them to sleep, at the very least. But how could he accomplish this?

He confided in Norman, as the Koala Elder.

'I don't see how you can possibly do this, David. But you're right, we all have to find a way to leave. I've prayed to the Great Spirit Koala for guidance, and I feel that this is what we should do. These people are bad, they're without shame, but the people they want to send us to are thoroughly, unspeakably evil, from what I understand.'

'What do you advise me to do, Norman?'

'Since you're already committed to escaping, let us all help you. Then the rest of us will follow as soon as we can. We'll create a diversion at one end of the enclosure – climbing onto the wire and jumping off again before we can be hit, and bellowing as loud as possible – while you climb the fence at the other end and make your escape. You will need to climb as you've never climbed before – so fast that you'll be over the fence in the blink of an eye – and then run as you've never run before. They'll call for others to come, and the enclosure may end up being surrounded... you'll have to get away before that can happen! And may the Great Spirit Koala protect you!'

....

David ran and ran, never looking back, until he was exhausted. As far as he could tell, he hadn't been followed, but he couldn't be completely sure. He would have liked to rest, yet he kept going, more and more slowly as his energy ebbed.

Eventually he was forced to sleep. But then he set off again....

That buffoonery with his captors had actually proved good exercise for him: he was fitter than he'd been in a long time.

Days went by. He became weaker and weaker, but he kept going, only stopping when he could no longer resist sleep.

Then he came to a river. 'If they have followed me', he thought, 'I can lose them by crossing this water, I'm sure. If only I wasn't so tired....'

David wasn't used to swimming; however, he knew he had to try. He counted to five, and dove in.

....

Giles and Bertie and their respective wives, Priscilla and Gwendolyn, happened to be boating on the very same river that David had jumped into.

'I say, it's a strange little furry creature, and it's swimming this way!' exclaimed Bertie.

'Oh, do help him, Bertie!' said Gwendolyn. 'He looks like he's in trouble.'

David was indeed in trouble; he didn't feel he could swim much further, and if he didn't swim, he'd drown.

Bertie and Giles went to the side of the boat, scooped David up as he swam near, and gently lifted him on board. David was too weak to even try to resist.

David shook off some water. He then sat down and looked around him.

'Oh, he's so *sweet*!' said Priscilla.

'He's *divine*!' said Gwendolyn.

'How do you know it's a *he*?' asked Giles.

'Well, he just looks like a male... um, furry thingy', said Priscilla.

'A sweet male furry thingy', echoed Gwendolyn.

David sighed. He wasn't a thingy, he was an animal, a sentient being, a living creature.

'By George, I believe the *thingy* sighed!' said Giles. 'I bet he's cold as well as wet.'

'Here, dear little thingy!' With this, Gwen took off her shawl and arranged it around David.

'By George, I think he's one of those *koala* thingies', said Giles. 'I've never seen one in the flesh, but I have seen pictures of them, and that's exactly what he looks like. Yes, indeed.'

'I don't care what he's called, he's just a very, very sweet furry thingy!' enthused Priscilla.

'Oh, yes, very, *very* sweet!' echoed Gwendolyn. She reached out her hand and gingerly stroked David's head.

David didn't flinch, let alone try to scratch her. He sensed that these people meant him well. They'd saved his life, after all.

'Oh, Gwennie, let's adopt him!' cried Priscilla, who also began stroking David.

'Oh yes, Prissie, yes, yes, yes!

Both Giles and Bertie sighed. Their respective homes already boasted dogs, cats, rabbits, guinea pigs, hamsters, hedgehogs... not to mention peacocks, swans and guinea fowl. Fortunately, they were sufficiently well-to-do that their homes had extensive grounds and large gardens, as well as many rooms. Both couples had an interest in botany, so that their gardens contained large varieties of trees, shrubs, bushes and flowers. (As luck had it, they even possessed eucalyptus trees, and as soon as David was to catch sight of one of the gum trees he climbed it, weak as he was, and ate.)

'So, which one of us gets to keep this sweet furry thingy?' Priscilla asked Gwen.

'We can share him! How about week and week about?'

'Super!'

The men sighed. But actually they thought David was a plucky little fellow, and much preferred him to some of their other pets... a few of which were scarcely *pets* at all, like those irritable, not to say *nasty* swans. They'd peck you as soon as look at you.

....

Within a short while, David began to sense that something was *odd*. The way Giles, Priscilla, Bertie and Gwen dressed, for example, seemed quite unlike anything he'd seen before; they also talked differently. This could have been due to a number of reasons, of course. But as the days and weeks went by, the oddities mounted up.

What he only gradually started to realise was that the river he'd jumped into was The River of Time, and that he'd entered a different time-zone.

It was a different century, in fact. If he had been human, he'd probably have heard rumours: that the river was haunted; that it caused madness; that people mysteriously appeared and disappeared from it. Rowing across it was considered safe; swimming in it was not.

It came to him eventually: *they were all dead*, everyone he'd known in the past; for they had to be. All the koalas: including Norman... and the strange koala who somehow knew about artists and art critics... and even his beloved Doreen.

All the humans, too: those who had captured him and the other koalas, and all those from the compound – though he didn't care about any of them.

They were the past, and he was now living in the future!

He felt a bizarre, dizzying combination of despair, bewilderment and elation. Despair, because he knew that all those koalas he'd cared about were gone; bewilderment, because it all seemed so strange; and elation, because his captors were all dead and could never hurt him again.

....

Priscilla made David a little pair of striped pyjamas (jimjams or jammies, as she called them). She had to help him into and out of them. At first David wasn't pleased, and growled a little....

'Oh, come on, my little furry thingy', cajoled Priscilla. 'Wear your little jimjams for mummy!'

'Ah well', sighed David to himself. 'These people may well be silly', he thought, 'with their silly ways of talking and even rather silly names for each other... not to mention their *jimjams*. But they're also nice people. Good, in fact. And goodness brings wisdom in time. Or hopefully so!'

....

Soon after David came to live at Priscilla and Giles' estate on alternate weeks, one of their many cats, a shorthair tortoiseshell named Doreen, took a fancy to him. That she was called Doreen was not lost on David. They would go to sleep together, curled around each other, purring and softly growling and grunting in furry comfort.

....

A little needs to be said here, perhaps, about David's hosts.

Giles had studied ancient Greek, and occupied himself with translating the Pre-Socratic philosophers. He went around the house – his and Priscilla's house, or anyone else's – declaiming his versions of Heraclitus, Parmenides and Empedocles. For a change, he would declaim other people's translations of the early Greek philosophers. For this reason, he was not always a popular guest, and sometimes not even a popular host (though David for one didn't mind his declaiming at all). Most people liked him for his good nature, however.

Priscilla was a painter, in oils, gouache and watercolour, and she found David to be an ideal subject, for not only did he sleep a great deal of the time, but he would also obligingly sit still for her when awake. You might think that because of this we might possess any number of faithful likenesses of him. Such is not the case. Although she wasn't an inept artist, Priscilla was unfortunately – in this regard, at least – a follower of successive Modernist "isms", including Pointillism, Postimpressionism, Cubism and Vorticism, and ending with Geometric Abstractionism; so that none of her paintings give us much idea of how David actually looked. In some he is largely dissolved into coloured dots; in others, there are very general koala-like shapes; and in the final pictures, if he'd been the model at all you could not have guessed it: rectangles, circles and triangles in various colours were all one could see.

Gwendolyn wrote short stories and novels. Her concern with women's rights and, more to the point with regard to her writing, "the image of women in our literature", as she tended to put it, had caused her to decide to make all her fictional characters female: not a single male made an appearance. This was in spite of her genuine liking for men – or some men, at least. She had no sexual interest in other women herself, and couldn't seem to write about sexual relations between women; the result was that her stories and novels had been unkindly referred to by one critic as "secular nunnery fiction". As her narrations were confined to a single character's consciousness, only ever revealing what she, the character, might see, hear, feel, think and know, the same unkind critic had said that reading her work was "like floating in the stream of consciousness of a secular nun".

Bertie was a diarist, whose work was an attempt at recording social occasions with his wife and their intellectual friends, on the one hand, and examining his own innermost thoughts and emotions – his soul, if you like – on the other. Apparently it was rather like some curious mixture of the Goncourt Brothers and Amiel's *Intimate Journal.*

I say "apparently", because nothing of it remains. Bertie was such a perfectionist that, much to the consternation of his wife and friends, he destroyed whatever he wrote within a few days.

....

Priscilla and Giles and Gwen and Bertie enjoyed entertaining guests, and having them to stay; and as they thought of themselves as intellectuals and artists, their invitations were for a certain elite. They weren't snobs, as such, though some of their friends and acquaintances certainly were.

Most of their visitors came from London for the weekend or for a few days, sometimes for longer. Over the years, Priscilla, Giles, Gwen and Bertie had become famous and highly regarded for their hospitality.

David became a great favourite with many of their guests.

David liked most of them. But a few he didn't.

There was one couple in particular... David liked *him*, but he didn't like *her*.

'Good little chap', the man, who was called Leonard, said, patting him on the head. He was a little condescending, perhaps, but he seemed to mean well.

He smiled at David and patted his head again. 'Would the furry little thingy like some water?' he asked. 'We're all having drinks, after all.'

'*Thingy* again!' thought David. But still, the man was clearly friendly.

'He's a *koala*, Leonard', said Giles. 'He came all the way from *Australia*... heavens knows how he got here. We found him trying to swim a river, quite a large one, you know. Plucky little fellow!'

'I'll get you some water, dear little furry thingy', said Gwen.

Leonard's wife was called Virginia. She had a long, slender face, and looked elegant and rather weary.

'In 1910 the world changed irrevocably', Virginia was saying. 'The world changed for me when I was taken from my native land,' thought David, 'and then again when I jumped into that river.'

'Or rather, *human relations* changed....'

Virginia and David had been looking askance at each other all evening (at least as far as a koala *can* look askance). David hopped up on a chair next to her and attempted to look even more askance. He just didn't like her, though he wasn't sure why, and it had become obvious to him that the feeling was mutual.

'I've been thinking of writing a novel from the viewpoint of a *dog*!' Virginia said. 'Not just any dog, mind you.... Elizabeth Barrett Browning's dog, Flush.'

'How very extraordinary!' exclaimed Giles. 'I *wonder* about the idea of writing about our lives from the viewpoint of a pet koala?'

'Oh, I don't think so!' said Virginia. She blew cigar smoke at David and made a quip about how vulgar Australians tended to be. David left the room almost immediately.

'The birds will speak in Greek to you', he said when he was out of hearing and heading for his own little room.

....

Another time, two brothers and a sister came to stay at Gwen and Bertie's: Osbert, Sacheverell and Edith, all of whom were writers.

'*Sacheverell?*' thought David. 'Priscilla! Now Osbert… and Sache-verell! What's wrong with people that they have to use weird names for their children! I think I'd rather be called Turnip.'

Osbert was casting an eye on David.

'Have I ever told you the pet beaver story?' he asked no one in particular.

'Yes!' the others chorused.

'Yes, Osbert, you have, he chewed up the antique furniture to make a dam in the living room!' said Bertie.

'Yes, that's right. I'm afraid they don't make good pets. Not like this little fellow!'

David was cuddling up to Gwen as Osbert spoke. He'd come to love Gwen and Priscilla, especially, as much as they loved him.

'Pavlick!' Edith suddenly exclaimed. 'I'm sure he loves me. I'm so sure of it!' She fluttered her hands and ring-adorned fingers. Her rings were indeed extraordinary, so she had cause to draw attention to them.

The others inwardly sighed. This had been going on for a long time. Her painter friend Pavel, or Pavlik as he was often called, was gay and involved with another man; poor Edith was deluding herself. Besides, she was a poet, and didn't she claim that poets shouldn't marry? No one could imagine her simply having *an affair*.

All this was lost on David; he was bored, and decided to go to sleep.

…….

All sentient beings die some day, and David was a sentient being (rather than a "sweet furry thingy").

As the years passed, he began to move more slowly, as age ensnared him, and he showed less interest in the things around: his natural and domestic surroundings, the animals and birds, and the people he lived with and their friends.

No one blamed him. But they were sad – Priscilla, Giles, Gwen and Bertie, especially – as they saw him lapse into a melancholy old age. His feline friend Doreen had passed on, and he missed her grievously... almost as much as her koala namesake.

And then one day Gwen, having realised she hadn't seen him for longer than usual, went to wake him and found him lying rigid in death.

....

There is a photograph of Gwen, Priscilla, Bertie and Giles in which, in one corner, there is a blurred shape in the shadows that might *just possibly* be a koala.

Why there aren't any clear photographs of David, I really don't know: I wish there were.

What would his eyes say to mine, if such an image did exist? Perhaps nothing; but possibly a great deal.

Or even better: a home movie.

Imagine: a koala's tongue lapping water from a proffered bowl; with the water drenching his chin fur. His avid, gentle eyes, amber with black pupils

3.

What was the fate of the other Herne Bay koalas? No one seems to know. There are stories, however.

Some say they also managed to escape. Some say they perished under the knife, after being kept in tiny cages and injected with this serum and that, forced to eat unfamiliar and unsatisfactory food or else starve, and otherwise experimented on: victims to the cause of "science".

If they did escape, the koalas didn't survive long; for Herne Bay never became known for having resident koalas. And outside of the compound, they would not have found suitable food.

Even the eucalyptus trees in the compound must have died.

Without a doubt the Herne Bay colony was closed down. But there is little agreement about when this happened, although it would seem highly likely that it was soon after David had escaped.

Eventually nothing was left but stories about the Herne Bay koalas.

....

How did the story of David and the other koalas come down to us?

It's all been a matter of rumours. (Or at least, this has been the case until very recently.)

We don't know quite how, but it seems that these rumours eventually reached Australia.

A number of Australian writers are said to have thought about depicting the troubles of the Herne Bay koalas, though nothing ever eventuated.

Rumours of rumours, then.

(Did any English writers even contemplate such a task? Not as far as I've been able to discover.)

Marcus Clarke may well have been the first writer to consider a novel about the Herne Bay koalas. This was some 70 years or so after the events, but nothing much, whether story or poem, appears to have been seriously entertained before this. Given his powerful treatment of the fate of English convicts in Australia, *For the Term of His Natural Life*, Clarke would likely have done the subject considerable justice. Unfortunately, even if he did intend to write such a work, as the rumours suggest, he left nothing of the sort behind at his early death in 1881.

Later, in 1918 or thereabouts, the artist and writer Norman Lindsay may well have thought of a sombre children's book about the Herne Bay koalas, as a follow-up of a kind to his successful and light-hearted book *The Magic Pudding*. Such are the rumours, at least. If he did, it's perhaps a good thing he changed his mind, or at any rate failed to go through with it. As an anti-Semite, he might well have insisted that the Herne Bay colony was an example of Jewish infamy... whereas as far as I know, none of the principals involved in setting it up were Jews.

(As it happens, a copy of *The Magic Pudding* had come into the hands of Priscilla and Giles, and Priscilla had read it to David. David had been staggered by the idea of a koala protagonist called Bunyip Bluegum. 'Bunyip Bluegum!' he'd thought. 'That's an even worse name than Sacheverell!')

Other writers have been cited... C J Dennis, for one... and there is even a story that the rather arcane and erudite, Symbolist-influenced poet Christopher Brennan mulled over the idea of a long poem imagining David's adventures after his escape, entitled *The Furry Wanderer*. If so, he was presumably prevented by his descent into alcoholism and depression in later years. Personally, I suspect the entire story is a rather obscure joke at Brennan's expense.

....

A few years ago I started to have vivid dreams of koalas in captivity in Herne Bay – David, especially. Along with the various stories I've managed to collect over time, these dreams form the basis of my account in the preceding pages.

I believe in these dreams, which dovetail so well with the rumours that have circulated for so long.

My name is David. I am not, of course, David the koala. I do, however, admire him in certain ways... perhaps even identify with him a little.

David was small and weak, but he was also gutsy and resourceful. (In Giles and Bertie's words, he was "a plucky little fellow".) *Resourceful?* His plan to drug his captors wasn't practical, but he'd done his best to come up with a means of escape. And he'd managed to eat and drink his fill and grow stronger through his antics in the compound.

He was to prove resourceful in another way, too... an altogether different way.

....

A poet friend of mine, Laurie Duggan, comes from Australia but has been living in England for some years. Laurie heard that a strange item had come up for sale at Christie's, a collection of pieces of wood and bark with lettering scratched into them. 'It's a text by someone named David', he told me over a drink at The Lamb pub in central London, 'and apparently it tells the story of the Herne Bay koalas.'

The temptation was too great! I sold everything I could in order to acquire these... tablets, let's call them. To think that David had scratched his story onto them with his own claws! Much of David's story depends on his understanding English... but to think that he taught himself to write!

Most of my friends thought I was crazy.

But they were wrong, as you shall now see.

4.

A Story of Captivity

BY DAVID THE KOALA

This is all true. This is what I went through. This is what the other koalas went through. For all who were party to this or knew about it and did nothing: may the great spirit koala forgive you, even as you turn to dust! For I find that I cannot.

We had no warning. They suddenly appeared amongst us one day. We had seen men before. But these were different. They wanted to capture us, as many of us as possible. And they were without mercy.

I'd been curled up asleep next to the love of my life, a koala named Doreen. Other males had more than one mate, but Doreen and I only cared for each other. We were content: blissfully content.

We were awakened by shouts and curses, and by the hurt cries of koalas who were being knocked down from their trees. I felt a sharp pain, and found myself falling to the ground. Doreen had suffered the same fate, and was beside me where I fell.

I heard Norman the koala elder bellowing to us all, trying to make us take flight. He still bellowed as he was caught in a net and taken away.

Then I heard a most terrible thing, worse to me than anything else! 'Let's have some fun!' someone shouted, advancing on Doreen and brandishing a club, his face a hideous leer. I sprang at him, my claws at his

LEGS. HE YELPED, THEN KICKED OUT, CATCHING ME IN THE BELLY. I SCREECHED AND SCREECHED! I SAW DOREEN LOOK AT ME, WONDERING WHAT TO DO; THEN SHE NODDED TO ME, SHOWING SHE UNDERSTOOD MY INTENTIONS, AND RAN. I ROLLED OVER IN PAIN.

I NEVER SAW MY LOVE DOREEN AFTER THAT DREADFUL DAY.

I CANNOT BRING MYSELF TO EVEN ATTEMPT A DESCRIPTION OF THE SUFFERINGS WE ENDURED, THOSE OF US WHO HAD BEEN CAUGHT! SUFFICE TO SAY MANY PERISHED ON THE FATEFUL VOYAGE TO A DISTANT LAND, AND THE REST WERE HALF-DEAD AT THE END OF IT. FOR INDEED WE WERE CARRIED OVER WATER ON SOME HUGE VESSEL FOR A GREAT LENGTH OF TIME, AND WHEN WE WERE DRIVEN TO LAND— ONLY TO BOARD ANOTHER VESSEL, THOUGH MERCIFULLY FOR A MUCH SHORTER JOURNEY — WE FOUND IT LOOKED NOTHING LIKE OUR BELOVED HOME. *AND I WEPT AND SHRIEKED ON BEHOLDING THE UNWONTED LAND WHERE ARE MURDER AND WRATH....*

INDEED, OUR MISFORTUNES WERE NOT OVER, BY ANY MEANS.

THE BODIES OF THE DEAD KOALAS HAD BEEN BURNED BEFORE OUR SECOND JOURNEY. WE BELLOWED AND SCREAMED IN ANGUISH AT THE SIGHT, SO MANY FRIENDS AND RELATIVES GONE! NOT EVEN KILLED FOR FOOD. (THIS WE COULD MORE OR LESS UNDERSTAND— EVEN IF IT WAS NOT OUR OWN WAY OF LIFE.) WE WERE TREATED SOMEWHAT BETTER ON THAT SECOND VESSEL, AND MOST OF OUR REMAINING NUMBER SURVIVED. BUT WHAT AWAITED US AT THE END OF THE VOYAGE? FURTHER HARDSHIPS, FURTHER BITTER WOES! IMPRISONMENT; BEING PRODDED AND KNOCKED WITH STICKS; TAUNTS, THREATS, DARK WORDS....

OUR CAPTORS WERE MEAN WITH FOOD AND WATER, BUT I FOUND WAYS OF OBTAINING MORE OF BOTH, BY ACTING THE FOOL AND THUS ENTERTAINING THEM. SOME OF THE KOALAS

JEERED AT ME. IN TIME THEY ALL UNDERSTOOD: I WAS PLAYING A PART, AND PLANNING TO ESCAPE.

THEN ONE DAY I SAW HIM— *HIM*, THE TERRIBLE BEING WHO HAD CAPTURED ME AND SEPARATED ME FROM MY BELOVED DOREEN. I MADE AT HIM, CLAWING WITH ALL MY STRENGTH. THE GUARDS PULLED ME FROM HIM, AND I RAN AND HID AS BEST I COULD, FEARFUL OF REPRISAL. HE SHOUTED THAT WE WERE ALL DOOMED, AND THAT WE'D DIE HORRIBLY.

WITH THE HELP OF NORMAN AND THE OTHER KOALAS, WHO DIVERTED THE GUARDS' ATTENTION, I DID ESCAPE, CLAMBERING OVER THE WIRE FENCE.

I RAN AND RAN, RAN AND HID, AND RAN AGAIN, ONLY STOPPING FOR SLEEP.

AT LAST I CAME TO A RIVER, AND DECIDED TO SWIM IT. I'D NEVER DONE MUCH IN THE WAY OF SWIMMING, BUT I THOUGHT I COULD DO IT, AS WEAK AS I WAS BY THEN.

A BOAT PICKED ME UP, AND I WAS BROUGHT TO SAFETY.

I GAINED EVERYTHING, AND I LOST ALL.... FREEDOM WAS MINE, AND A HOME WITH THE PEOPLE WHO HAD RESCUED ME, AND WHO WERE KIND. BUT NEVER, NEVER AGAIN WOULD I SEE MY FELLOW KOALAS OR MY NATIVE LAND!

[The manuscript breaks off here, and does not resume.]

5.

Rest in peace, koala! Your story has been told and will live on.

TABITHA'S DILEMMA; OR: THE CAT WHO COULDN'T SLEEP

Tabitha had not been able to sleep for several days. Not a proper sleep, at any rate – only the occasional brief doze.

She tried counting mice: imaginary mice, I mean. One mouse, two mice, three mice, four mice.... However, all this did was to make her want to get up and hunt for a real mouse!

She'd taught herself to turn the radio in the living room on and off. It was permanently tuned to BBC3, which played all through the night. She had it on quietly, so that the sound didn't wake her owners. Listening to it didn't help her to sleep, but it did help to educate her. She felt that even if she was still an insomniac cat, she'd learned a thing or two. She'd listened to Bach, she'd listened to Dowland, she'd listened to Schubert lieder... and so much more.

Her owners, Bruce and Beryl, did notice that she was bleary-eyed and sluggish, and not at all as lively as normal, but decided that all she needed was a different sort of cat food.

That didn't help, however.

She confided in her friend Peterkins, an amiable and rather lazy ginger tom. Peterkins yawned, stretched himself, and said: 'You tabby females! Always something amiss. Ah, please don't think I lack sympathy. Cheer up now, I'm sure you'll get some real sleep soon. Have you tried a change of habits, I wonder?'

A change of habits? Tabitha thought about this, in between counting mice and getting up from her basket to look for a mouse.

Well, she liked sleeping, or at least trying to sleep, in warm, comfortable places... people's laps, her basket, somewhere in the sunshine.

'Instead of Bruce and Beryl's laps', she thought, 'why not their *feet*?' But this really was too uncomfortable to help her sleep, even when they were wearing slippers, and besides they shoved her away with cries of 'Silly cat!'

So she tried the refrigerator. When Beryl opened the fridge door for the last time that night (she was wearing her nightgown and clearly intended going to bed), Tabitha snuck in, and Beryl, not having realised, closed the door again.

The refrigerator was uncomfortable *and* cold. And claustrophobic, to boot: she was shut in, shut in, shut in, in a confined, dark space! Tabitha's teeth chattered, she began to ache, she felt as if she'd been buried alive. None of this helped her to sleep!

She meowed as loudly as she could, in the hope of being found and set free. Fortunately, Bruce came into the kitchen in search of a midnight snack; he heard Tabitha's cries, and quickly came to her aid. 'Silly, silly Tabitha!' he exclaimed. 'What on earth are you doing in *there*? Really, you *are* becoming strange. You'll be eating grass next!'

'Hmm', thought Tabitha, 'that's an idea! I could try changing my eating habits. But let's first get warm!'

So it was back to her basket. She didn't really sleep, of course, but she did doze a little.

The following day found her out in the garden, munching the grass. 'Oh dear', thought Tabitha, 'what awful muck!' She also nibbled some leaves, and even a few flowers. 'Yuck! Disgusting!' she said to herself. 'Oh well, perhaps all this will make me sleep.'

It didn't. All that happened was that she felt quite sick for a while.

Tabitha began to lose faith in her friend Peterkins' advice.

'Ah', said Peterkins, when she related what she'd been up to, 'you're not going far enough! Literally, in fact. I believe *a change of scenery* is what's required.'

'Hmm', thought Tabitha. 'Perhaps he's right!'

This was quite a step for Tabitha: normally she stayed close to home. Nevertheless, the very next day found her waiting at the bus-stop just down the road from her home. When the bus arrived and the doors opened, she hopped inside. Fortunately the driver didn't ask her for a pass or a fare.

Tabitha looked around and spied another cat – a handsome black and white tom – ensconced on a seat in full sunlight. He sleepily lifted one eyelid. 'Do you come here often?' the cat asked.

The bus was otherwise empty at this point, and the driver had her eyes on the road and appeared to be oblivious to them.

'It's my first time', said Tabitha.

'Well, my name's Milo, and let me fill you in on the situation here. Right off, since *I* was here first, this is *my* bus, and *I* give the orders! Now, you did admit you'd never been here before, so don't try to claim otherwise.'

'I wouldn't dream of it', said Tabitha.

'And don't worry about the driver! That's Molly, my owner, and she never notices *anything*!'

Just then the bus came to a halt.

'Hush!' said the tom, 'there are people getting on at this stop. I'll *show* you what to do!'

It was actually very simple and didn't require any showing. Milo was just... well, *showing off.*

You might call it begging for warmth and attention. And the occasional treat. Indeed, it was much the same as human begging, where someone goes around asking strangers for spare money, often spinning a hard luck story or otherwise playing on their good nature. In Tabitha and Milo's case, they used their feline charms so that people gave him titbits – a little something from a chicken or salmon sandwich, say – as well as petting them and letting them lie on their laps. The two cats looked pleadingly, they meowed softly and winningly, they purred, they rubbed around legs... anything to draw the right sort of attention.

Molly, indeed, didn't seem to care about any of this, or even notice.

At the end of the route, Tabitha gave Milo an appreciative sniff and he gave her one back. Then she jumped out of the open door of the bus and scampered off. Things might have turned out differently – a whirlwind romance, perhaps – except that Tabitha and Milo had both had visits to vets, and neither felt any interest in the opposite sex, at least as far as courtship and mating were concerned.

Tabitha didn't have any real idea of where she was going. But when she padded by a medical centre, she suddenly had an idea.

Since *her visit*, she didn't trust vets; but perhaps a doctor would be better? It seemed worth a try.

Now, Tabitha had never spoken – spoken, rather than meowed, yowled, wailed or purred – to anyone other than other cats. Not even Beryl or Bruce. It simply wasn't what cats do. Normally they pretend that they can't speak. It makes them seem more helpless and in need of being looked after. They confused things by certain displays of independence and by hunting, but basically they *were* cats after all.

However, this seemed to Tabitha a special case. She said the words to herself: 'It's a special case. A *special* case. I need to sleep! I need to do whatever it takes!'

A desperate decision on Tabitha's part: desperate and, yes, necessary.

She padded into the medical centre, sidled past the front desk, checked the directory on the wall, and then took the elevator to the second floor.

When she got there, she saw there was a long queue. 'Oh well', thought Tabitha, 'I'm in no hurry.' She rubbed around people's legs, sat on the odd lap. No one seemed to mind: the reverse, in fact. She had feline charm. She knew that.

At last the waiting room became empty, apart from Tabitha herself. Even the doctors and nurses had left, all except one doctor and one nurse. Tabitha knew this was her chance.

Then the last of the nurses left. 'Good night, doctor!' she called as she went out the door. She didn't seem to notice that Tabitha was still there. Tabitha took her chance, and entered the doctor's office.

'Oh, hello, puss!' a surprised and tired doctor said. 'What brings you here?'

'I need your help!' said Tabitha.

'You can *talk*!' he exclaimed, and promptly passed out. Fortunately he was sitting down when this occurred.

The doctor woke up with Tabitha on his lap.

'It's all right' said Tabitha. 'You're just dreaming. Say it to yourself: "It's all a dream. But I must treat this cat within the dream."'

'Mischievous cat! I know when I'm dreaming and when I'm not!'

'Well, it was worth a try' , said Tabitha. 'Heal me, physician! For I cannot sleep.'

'More and more interesting! You not only speak, you're an insomniac as well. This is a case for the medical journals!'

'I'll deny it all', said Tabitha. 'Or rather, I just won't do anything except purr and meow and pretend to sleep.'

'What a damned spoil sport! But why haven't you gone to a vet rather than come to me?'

So she explained. The doctor nodded in understanding. He seemed a decent sort, Tabitha thought.

'Well, unfortunately I can't really help you, puss. I could prescribe sleeping pills, but you'd never get the prescription filled, and besides, I don't know what effect they'd have on you. You might never wake up.'

'Hmm, I don't like the sound of *that*!'

'No, I'm sure you don't. You know, young lady, I think it's your *mind* that needs to be treated. Have you considered any form of mental or behavioural therapy?'

'This is all new to me, doc', said Tabitha, scratching her head. 'What would you suggest?'

'Perhaps you could join an encounter group! People get together to act out their anger and their anxieties and so forth, and yell and shout at each other, and then the leader of the group quietens them down and they all feel better. You know, I've often wondered about joining a group myself – it sounds such fun!'

Tabitha stretched herself and then jumped down from the doctor's lap.

'Not for me, I'm afraid, doc. I need something one-to-one.'

'Ah, yes, I see!' He got up, and then he stretched. Suddenly his face lit up. 'Why didn't I think of it before! A psychotherapist! We have one in this very building. Why don't you sleep here tonight, and I'll take you to see him in the morning.'

'Sleep! If only', said Tabitha.

'I *could* inject you with a sedative, but I'm not used to dealing with cats. You might not wake up from that, either.'

'Let's not, in that case. Say, doc, have you got anything to eat in this place? I'm getting a little peckish.'

Doctor Dave – for that was his name – could only find some milk, which had been left in a fridge in the staff relaxation room. He put it in a saucer for Tabitha and then left.

Tabitha didn't sleep that night, needless to say, though she did doze a little.

In the morning, Doctor Dave was, as good as his word, there early to escort Tabitha to the psychotherapist's office.

'Hello, Harold!' Doctor Dave exclaimed in greeting when they arrived there.

'Dave! Good to see you. Now, what have we here? Where did you get the pussycat?'

'Hello', said Tabitha. 'Can you help me to sleep?'

'Don't faint, Harold!' Doctor Dave shouted.

But Harold fainted anyway.

Doctor Dave managed to bring Harold round, and then explained the situation to the astonished therapist. Harold said that he didn't think there was much he could accomplish, especially as he wasn't used to treating cats, but that he'd do a trial session with Tabitha anyway.

'Lie down on the couch, please, and don't go to sleep', said Harold to Tabitha.

'No fear of that!' Tabitha replied.

'Dave, you'd better go now. I need to be alone with the patient.'

'I should go and attend to *my* patients, of course', said Doctor Dave, though he looked reluctant to leave. 'Goodbye, puss, I hope we'll meet again.'

'Goodbye, Doctor Dave. And thank you!'

For the next fifty minutes Tabitha talked about her life, while Harold listened and sometimes prompted her and also asked the occasional question. He took notes as well.

'So, you never knew your father, and you were separated from your mother and siblings when very young. That would explain quite a lot. And then "the visit", as you call it... no doubt that's led to subconscious sexual frustrations.'

'Don't talk dirty', said Tabitha. 'I'm just not romantically inclined towards toms anymore. Nor towards female pusses, in case that was going to be your next question!'

'Hmm', said Harold, getting up from his chair and beginning to pace. 'I can see causes for neurosis, though at the same time your story isn't very different from many other cats? These past events might be at the root of your insomnia... or on the other hand, they might not.'

'Can't you do *something* to help me?'

'Two years of therapy, one session a week except when I'm on holiday... that *might* help. But on the other hand it might not. Also, I'm not experienced in treating cats, as I said. And you couldn't pay me, anyway. Sorry, puss.'

'Oh, oh, oh!' exclaimed Tabitha. She began to yowl piteously.

Harold stopped pacing. 'Now, now, enough of that!' He put his hand to his chin and thought for a moment. 'Have you tried Zen meditation?' he asked.

'Never even heard of it', said Tabitha, calming herself down and eager to know if it might help her.

'Well, you'd have one-to-one sessions with a Master, who'd say unintelligible things to you – they're called *koans*. A bit like riddles, except dafter. You'd have to think about them, and then have further sessions. But the really important bit is the meditation itself. You'd sit in a hall or just a room for hours on end, amongst the other disciples, and try to empty your mind. And if you fell asleep, the Master would hit you across the shoulders with a stick.'

'THAT WOULDN'T HELP ME!' cried Tabitha. 'This is the best advice you can give?'

'I guess I wasn't *really* thinking', said Harold. 'Anyway, that's the end of your trial session. Sorry it wasn't of any real use. I suppose I can collect your fee from Doctor Dave. Goodbye, puss.'

Tabitha left in a thoroughly dejected mood.

She walked. And she walked. And then she stopped for a while, and then she walked some more.

Eventually she came to a large complex of buildings. In the courtyard she saw a number of young people: some of them were sitting and some were standing, some were talking and some were silent, and most of them were eating.

'I'm peckish!' thought Tabitha. 'Maybe I can beg some food.'

Indeed she did. Some of the young people ignored her; others however responded to her meows and pleading looks as well as her rubbing against their arms and legs, and gave her scraps of food as well as petting and patting her.

Tabitha didn't know it, but she'd found her way into a university, or at least one of its campuses. The young people were in fact students.

She made herself at home. She had nowhere else to go, for the present at least. She wasn't able to sleep at Bruce and Beryl's; neither could she sleep at Doctor Dave's surgery. 'Perhaps', thought Tabitha, 'I can sleep *here*.'

She wandered around the buildings, in and out of various halls and rooms. Lectures and seminars were going on, and Tabitha sampled them. She sat or lay on seats or chairs next to the students; sometimes she lay on their laps. She listened a little, got up and padded quietly out, and listened somewhere else.

Then something wonderful happened: during one of the lectures, when she was lying down by herself at the back of the hall, she fell into a sound sleep!

She'd seemed to hear the same phrases over and over, in one lecture or seminar after another: phrases such as "always already" (or was it "already always"?), "reading the text against itself", "simulacra and simulations", "the unconscious is structured like a language" and the like, almost always delivered in a droning voice. It was magical! The effect was hypnotic or, more precisely, soporific.

Tabitha once more became a contented cat. She no longer had any trouble sleeping.

The janitors fed her and petted her. Some of the students also fed and petted her. So did some of the secretaries, and the security people. Even a few of the lecturers followed suit; and one of them, skilled as an amateur in woodwork, made her a basket to sleep in.

Soon others – students, cleaners, secretaries, lecturers, security staff – were trying their hand at basket-making, and Tabitha had her choice of comfortable (and sometime not *quite* so comfortable) places to sleep. And sleep she did!

It couldn't last, of course.

'What's this cat doing here?' demanded the Head of English, stubbing his toe on one of Tabitha's baskets. Tabitha happened to be inside it, and woke up and meowed.

'Oh, she's our mascot!' exclaimed a female student. Others anxiously nodded their agreement.

'Not any more she isn't! *Felines don't belong here*! Little furry pest!'

So Tabitha was escorted to the entrance of the campus and shooed away.

'Not fair, not fair, not fair!' she thought to herself, and began to yowl as she sadly padded away.

Just then she heard a familiar voice cry out: 'It's Tabitha! Look, it's our Tabitha!'

'Oh, it's my Bruce and Beryl', thought Tabitha.

Now, you may be wondering how Bruce and Beryl came to be there. They were engaged in shopping therapy, to take their minds off Tabitha's disappearance. Near to the university was the 24th largest shopping mall in the whole of Europe. Or was it the 25th? It was a very large and famous shopping mall, at any rate.

'We've looked for you everywhere! There are "missing" posters on half the trees in our suburb. And here you are! Where have you been, you naughty cat?'

'Oh, Bruce, she may have been *kidnapped*, for all we know, and only just escaped! After all, I don't think she could have come all this way by herself.'

Tabitha purred and rubbed herself around their legs.

'Ah! Are you this miserable feline's owners?' It was the Head of English, who had followed Tabitha to make sure she was really gone. (Apparently he had nothing better to do with his time.)

'*Miserable?*' exclaimed Bruce. 'She's a sweet, loving cat. Don't you dare call her "miserable"!'

'This flea-ridden piece of fur? She's driven my staff and students to making baskets for her with her winning ways, the manipulative little scoundrel, and no doubt given all of us fleas!'

'Tabitha is a clean cat', said Beryl. 'Don't you insult her!'

'Good for you both', thought Tabitha. She scratched herself.

'See! See!' cried the Head of English.

'You're just making her nervous!' said Beryl. 'Come, dear Tabitha.

Don't listen to the nasty man.'

Bruce and Beryl took her home.

At first, Tabitha was worried that she'd go back to her sleeping problems. But her problems were over. She found that she just had to call to mind those droning voices and those soporific phrases, and off to sleep she went.

Sleep well, Tabitha! Your insomniac days and nights are no more.

LIONEL'S STORY

L ionel yawned, rather elaborately.

However, I knew he wasn't bored; it was just that it was a hot, drowsy afternoon in the Central African savannah.

In fact, I also yawned, though less elaborately.

Lionel noticed and nodded to me.

'I'll begin now', he said in his gravelly voice. 'It was the music that first attracted us. Simply, it was the most beautiful thing any of us had ever heard! There had been sounds, similar sounds, coming from the house before.... *This* was different, though!'

Lionel paused, and then closed his eyes. He began to sing, in his gruff bass voice. I recognised the melody, but his singing took a little getting used to, let us say. Feodor Chaliapin he most definitely wasn't. However, it was clear that he loved the music greatly, and this touched me.

He stopped singing, and paused again.

'I was quite young', he resumed, 'and I suppose my enthusiasm got the better of me. We'd all moved as close to the house as possible, and I just couldn't help myself: I started singing along with the music, or at least *trying* to.'

'And Albert heard you?'

'Yes, he heard me, and stopped playing. He and his friend – the owner of the house, who I'm sorry to say was only an indifferent musician himself, and who we'd heard playing previously – came out to investigate. Albert was wearing a black coat and trousers, with a white shirt, and his friend was wearing a grey coat and trousers and a white shirt. They both looked startled. They seemed even more startled when we cried out: 'More! Play more!' Albert shook that great head of his with the bushy white hair and moustache, and said something to his companion which we couldn't catch. But then he turned to us, smiled and said: "Yes! I'll play for you!" '

'That must have been quite a moment', I ventured.

'Ah, indeed it was. Our lives were never the same.'

'And it really was the music that caused such a difference in your lives?'

'Sebastian's music? As Albert played it for us? Oh, yes!

'In the first instance, anyway.

'But you also have to remember what Albert's like as a person! How he thinks, what he says, even just how he *is*.'

He got up and stretched, walked about a little and then lay down again.

'Can you say a bit more about the music and how it affected you?' I asked.

'There was a sense of joy, yet also sadness – and sometimes both together; and these feelings, these combined feelings, especially, somehow made me want to change my life! My heart was struck in that way! And more than anything else, there was a promise of peace in that music – peace such as I had never known!

'The others felt this, too. We were overcome... subdued at the end of the performance, because we felt so overcome.'

Lionel's words made me think of the poet Rilke, his 'Archaic Torso of Apollo', to be precise. But it didn't seem worth pursuing this with Lionel. We were talking about music, not sculpture. And yet, there was the same charge, for Rilke and for Lionel: one must change one's life.

What I did say to him was that for me it was the brilliant structuring of the music with deep emotion at the same time that was significant. And a very real spirituality.

'*Spirituality?*' queried Lionel.

'In a sense it's going beyond – or feeling that you've been taken beyond – everything around you, and also beyond yourself... and yet in another sense it's going further into these things, deep down, and further....'

'I hate paradoxes, don't you?' asked Lionel. 'They're so irritating!'

'Yes', I replied. 'Yet we can't seem to do without them.'

'I suppose so', said Lionel, getting to his feet, stretching, and walking around a little. He then lay down again. The sun had moved, and he'd moved, too, to a new patch of shade.

I was still thinking about how I might explain what I meant by "spirituality".

'I'd also say it's about moving towards a great harmony and a feeling of glory in that harmony. Anything discordant becomes resolved in it, because all that's simply dross is dissolved.'

'*Dross?*' queried Lionel, raising his head to look directly at me.

'Dross... it's a cliché, I suppose, an overused expression.... But it refers to what's negative, distasteful, impure....'

'Do you mean like *hyenas?*'

'Well, not quite....'

'Have you ever met a *nice* hyena? Let me put it another way... have you ever seen one *eating*? If you had, you'd know what they're like! Yuk! Couldn't *they* just dissolve?'

'Certain people have claimed to find Sebastian's music – or some of it, at least – dry and abstract', I said, in an attempt to divert him from the subject of hyenas. I was thinking of late works like 'The Musical Offering' and 'The Art of Fugue', especially – though personally I don't agree with this judgement in the least.

'Don't they have ears?' asked Lionel rhetorically, his voice becoming a loud growl. 'DON'T THEY HAVE HEARTS?'

He shook his thick mane of hair and looked me full in the eyes. I admit he looked terrifying at that moment.

'Well, I can only say they're fools', I said.

'Yes', he said, visibly calming down again. I inwardly sighed with relief.

'You became a vegetarian, didn't you?' I asked, hoping now to get him off the subject of Sebastian's music, or rather, those who dislike some at least of it.

'Ah, yes! Eventually, through Albert, I came to see the animals and birds we'd always hunted – zebra, eland, hartebeest, kudu, heron – as beautiful and precious. "Reverence for life" was Albert's way of summing up how he felt, and we gradually found ourselves taken hold of by this.

'As Albert said, he didn't eat meat, nor did large creatures like elephants, hippos, rhinos, gorillas, water buffalos or giraffes. *Did we really need to?*'

I'm not a vegetarian, though I didn't feel like admitting it. I just nodded, as if in agreement.

'We never thought of ourselves as *predators* or *killers*', Lionel continued, 'though we were. It was simply how we lived, and how our ancestors had lived. And it's not that we enjoyed inflicting pain. It was survival... the only way we thought we *could* survive.

'We did think of ourselves as *hunters*. We hunted – we scavenged, too – in order to eat, and we ate to keep on living. That other creatures died because of us seemed simply a matter of course. It didn't keep any of us awake when we wanted to sleep.'

Lionel paused.

'We became confused, oh so confused... enriched by the music, yet conflicted and dissatisfied as well! Dissatisfied with our lives.'

He paused again, this time for so long that the silence became strained... terribly strained.

Then he got to his feet, stretched and yawned.

'I think that's enough for today!' he said as he began to walk away.

'But tomorrow?'

'Yes, I'll be back here tomorrow!'

'Ah!' I exclaimed.

....

Most years, usually at the same time of year, Albert travelled in secret from his hospital and home in Lamberéné, in the region of Gabon, to stay with a close friend named Peter, in or rather near a village some-

where in Cameroon. (When I later talked with Albert about Lionel, I was asked not to disclose the specific whereabouts – for the same reason that Albert travelled there secretly: it was his retreat, where he could have quiet and rest. And even now, I will not betray a promise. Everyone deserves a measure of privacy in their life, and also about their life.)

Peter, who was a semi-recluse, had installed a pedal piano in his home, much like the one Albert played in Lamberéné. A pedal piano? Yes, a rather curious instrument, sometimes known as a piano-organ: it's equipped with a pedalboard for bass notes that are played with the feet. Organists take to it like proverbial ducks to water. As Lionel said, Peter played it indifferently, if truth be told, but Albert had been renowned for his keyboard playing – the organ, especially – long before he came to Africa.

I'm an optician and a writer. I make my living as an optician, but writing is my real love. I'd made my way to Lamberéné in the vague hope of helping Albert in or with his hospital, the same as many others have felt the call to help this great doctor and humanitarian... and musician.

I discovered I was not cut out for it.

The room I was given was cramped and uncomfortable. When I asked an assistant at the hospital about better accommodation, I was stared at in consternation and disbelief. 'There isn't any! The rooms are all alike!' I was told.

I didn't think I'd have any qualms about lepers, but I was mistaken. I guess I'm an aesthete... or I don't have enough empathy and compassion. Which might even amount to the same thing, in my case at least.

And the mosquitoes! Don't get me started on that subject. Or the heat! We all had to wear pith helmets whenever we went out, to avoid getting sunstroke.

Although eating meat wasn't forbidden, I felt I'd look more worthy in Albert's eyes if I stuck to vegetables at communal meal-times. I was desultorily playing with some lettuce with my fork when Albert pushed his own bowl of lentil soup my way, with a kindly smile. I didn't dare tell him I hated lentils!

More importantly than any of this, my services as an optician were nothing like as in demand as I'd thought, and if they had been, there wasn't the equipment for eye tests or the lenses and frames, anyway.

My skills as a writer were, it seemed, even less required. (Admittedly, my main field of literary endeavour is avant-garde poetry, and even the few essays I've written have been deemed "esoteric".)

Then, when I was about to give up altogether, I had a dream, a dream so vivid that I knew it had to be true.

It sealed my departure.

But I had not given up, not really. I had simply changed my means of support. Even if I knew I couldn't publish what I planned to write for some time to come... years, possibly.

I was leaving for Cameroon.

......

Lionel was as good as his word, as the saying goes. I found him waiting for me the next morning, lying down in the shade.

'We used to eat our young. Did you know that?' he asked abruptly.

I was too taken aback to speak. 'Ah, I'm sorry! I've shocked you. I should perhaps explain: if a male felt that the offspring presented to him by his partner weren't really his, but another male's, he'd eat them, right in front of her.'

'I *am* shocked', I said.

'I'm not defending the practice! I just wanted to make clear to you how we lived. It was the first thing Albert persuaded us to stop doing.'

He paused, flicking his tail.

'Do you ever regret your decision to stop eating meat?' I asked. 'Is it difficult being a vegetarian lion?'

Lionel yawned elaborately.

'Ah', he said, 'you do get used to it. It was difficult at first; of course it was! But I'd never go back to my old ways; and neither would the others in my pride.'

He paused for so long that I began to think he'd lost interest.

'And this is because – ' , I started to say.

'You've met Albert!' he interrupted me. 'He inspired us with the gifts of gentleness, pity, and respect for others. If we turned back to our old ways, we'd be betraying him! And we'd be betraying the beauty, the beautiful spirit, of that wonderful music he brought us!'

We were both silent for a while. I confess I hoped he wasn't going to start singing again: once was really enough.

'You know', I said at last, 'I've always wanted to....' I trailed off in embarrassment.

'Touch a lion's mane?'

'How on earth did you know?'

'Well, there are a lot of things I've discovered about you humans over the past few years. Go on, do it. I won't bite!'

I reached out my hand.

The next thing I knew was that I was lying on my back and coming to after I don't know how long. Lionel was standing over me. I hate to say this, but his breath was rank.

'Sorry', he said. 'Just a reflex action. But I only batted you.'

'In a boxing match with Sonny Liston, I'd bet on you!' I said.

Lions don't laugh or even smile. This can sometimes be disconcerting.

'I didn't understand that at all!' he finally said. 'A *what*? With *whom*?'

I explained what boxing was, and that Liston was at present, that is, in 1963, the heavyweight champion of the world and an extremely formidable puncher.

'I'm sure Albert wouldn't approve of all that', he said sadly, shaking his great head. 'But never mind. If you still want to, go ahead and touch. I won't hit you this time.'

I ran my fingers through his mane. It was exquisite, just as I thought it would be.

'Have you thought of what this story should be called?' he suddenly asked.

'I think I'll call it "A Timeless Golden Triangle: Schweitzer, Bach and Lionel".'

'Perhaps a little too... *involved*?' he queried. 'Why not just call it "Lionel's Story"? But I don't want to influence you. You're the writer. It's *your* story now.'

But it is, of course, Lionel's story. And unlike my other literary endeavours, I've tried to write simply and straightforwardly.

......

I went back there a few years later. Albert had died by then.

There was no sign of Lionel or his pride. I assume they'd all died, too. They may have been killed, in one way or another. Some of them may have died of old age.

Perhaps the new diet failed them in the end, even if it had seemed to work for some while.

Or perhaps they died of heartbreak when Albert passed away, such was their love for him.

Hail and farewell, dear Lionel! May your great heart be at peace.

A FINAL WAVE

I've journeyed here again, along a route I never remember yet always follow, never clear except in the instance, yet always there. It's only a short distance now to the sea, with its waves breaking over rocks, cliffs high above, and only an equally short walk in the other direction to the town, with its arcades, shops, cafés and public houses... and then hills in the distance.

In my hotel room: a yellow flower in a glass globe. And caught within the glass: iridescent drops, tiny globules of light.

I arrived late, yet just in time for a meal: cheese and bacon omelette, salad on the side. Not bad at all.

I'm promised waffles for breakfast.

Lashing rain has been my lot ever since arriving here. *Flagellating.*

A young woman sits in the branches of a tree. As I approach, she calls out: 'Listen!' So I sit down on the wet grass and listen.

' "I'll catch you!" cried the mother koala, as her joey fell from the bough. "Here", said the bear, scooping the crow out of water festooned with weeds onto the bank and then walking away; the crow was too astonished to say anything. "I'll speak now", exclaimed the stone. And it began its story...'

Suddenly she jumps down, and just as suddenly I lose consciousness. I wake up with a headache and a bump on the head: presumably due to a kick which somehow I never saw.

Sheet lightning tonight.

'Oh, *her*! She's a crazy one, she is. One of those animal rights activists, and more.'

'Camps out somewhere in the hills. Or so I've heard.'

'She's a fierce one. As well as being strange. *Dead* strange, I'd say.'

I notice a jukebox in a corner of the pub: one of the old-fashioned kind, large and brightly painted, decorated with flashing lights. There are a couple of Randy Newman songs, 'Sail Away' and 'Small People', and I play them both.

When I go the bar, the publican says, 'No one likes that second song you played. It never gets played by any of *us*. We've been meaning to remove it.'

I notice for the first time that he's standing on a little platform behind the bar.

As the great jazz musician Lester Young used to say, *I can feel a draught.*

Waves rising, washing, spreading over the rocks at the base of the cliff and the path I'm walking on, wetting my feet despite my shoes. (Why didn't I bring boots? I ask myself.)

When I reach the top, and walk some ways, I'm astonished to suddenly encounter a troop of baboons: what on earth are they doing here? One of them runs up to me and seems inclined to be friendly; I sense no danger and feel no fear, though this changes when some orang-utans pass by, carrying planks of wood and, more worryingly, hammers and saws. The baboons don't seem concerned, so I try to appear indifferent, though my heart's beating fast. Then I remember that I've heard something about an experiment in these parts, called

The Barque Project....

I enter a pub and there she is! "The wild girl", as I think of her.

I sit down opposite her. 'Murder has been committed here', she says, without the least prompting. And then gets up and leaves.

'The cliffs are haunted! No one goes there, apart from the bloody animals. Didn't you see the sign?'

'I saw something that said, EE UT. Afraid I didn't take much notice of it.'

'That was KEEP OUT! Some of the letters have faded away, that's all.'

'We don't go up there', someone else says, 'but the animals come down here when they think it's safe. Poaching. And stealing! They even steal lumber!'

'Now, that's probably gypsies', says the publican.

'Gypsies, my eye! There haven't been Romanies around here for decades.'

I don't mention that I've seen orang-utans carrying planks. It isn't any business of mine.

'Anyway, when the animals come down from the cliffs, we have a chance to grab them!'

'That's right', another says. 'We caught one of those big ginger-haired apes once – '

'Orang-utans', I say. 'Reddish-brown hair, actually.'

'Whatever! Anyway, we tied it to a pole and threw rotten fruit and vegetables at it, then eggs, then rocks and stones. It was utterly hysterical, right up to the time it died – and we were in hysterics.'

I take my drink to a table of my own in a far corner.

To my even greater surprise than before, the wild girl joins me. She'd evidently been sitting in the shadows somewhere in the pub.

'I hate humans', she says viciously. *'And that includes you.'* She finishes her drink, and abruptly leaves.

I've been doing a little research.

Orang-utans are possibly the gentlest of the ape family, as well as amongst the most intelligent.

But even if the townsfolk didn't know this, any more than I had, their attitudes and behaviour were disgusting and grotesque.

An emotional numbing? Emotional blindness, so to speak? (Or is this insulting to the blind?) A refusal, conscious or unconscious, to see that we're fellow sentient creatures: able to feel pain and, yes, have feelings? Or a deliberate decision to be cruel, where you can, usually, with animals, rather than where you most often can't, that is, with other people – without recompense, at any rate?

I remember – from when I was a boy – my mother trying to remonstrate with our next door neighbour, who allowed his son to pluck the feathers from live birds. He seemed to think it amusing that Mum would care.... The cries distressed and haunted me.

A little more research: I find that The Barque Project was founded by a female philanthropist and animal-lover, who recruited occasional help from volunteers to establish a sanctuary where a variety of animals, including carnivores, were raised to co-exist peacefully, both with each other and with the project's workers, and to roam freely along the cliff tops. Some of the animals, such as the orang-utans, were also taught certain skills: in particular, basic carpentry. Just how far the experiment had succeeded and developed is open to speculation. But two things were clear: first, the townsfolk had opposed the project right from the beginning; and second, the founder had mysteriously disappeared, her disappearance surrounded by rumours of foul play, although no proof of this has ever come to light.

'Haven't heard that name in quite a long time! She left here some years back.'

I point out that the philanthropist only vanished two years ago, according to the reports I've been reading.

'Ah yes, that's right: I remember now, it was *two* years ago when she left.'

'And she should have taken those bloody animals with her!' someone adds.

The weather only gets worse. I'm a fool to venture out at all.

At the far end of town: 'We are inbred, it's true!'

'And proud of it! No outsiders will taint *our* gene pool!'

I won't return to that particular pub, either.

Up on the cliffs again, I decide to explore further than before. But once I've reached a certain point, I'm met by groups of baboons, orang-utans and gorillas, all blocking my path. They don't try to attack me, but it's clear they do not want me to continue along this way. I turn and go back.

Newscasters on TV, computers and radio tell us of travail globe-wide: gales, storms, floods, hurricanes, tsunamis....

'Heavy rain in deserts, even...', someone comments.

'*Something to do with polar ice caps? Icebergs melting?* What a lot of tosh! Icebergs don't bloody well melt. And what if they *did?*'

'If you believe that, you'll believe anything! Bloody so-called ethnic cleansing, for example. Just fucking propaganda!'

'So what's wrong with being clean, anyway?'

'Bloody cry-babies! And then Liberal softies get on the case!'

'Fucking Commies, too! Should all be destroyed, like the scum they are!'

'No, that's not what it's about! There's *nothing real* to it at all. It just never really happens! Smoke and mirrors.'

'Like the Gulf War! Oh, come on! Fucking media rubbish!'

Fortunately there are still a couple of other pubs in this town I can try....

Broadcasting has now ceased... or at least, nothing is being received here, not anymore; possibly never again? The last I heard was that wherever less threat and actual harm prevailed, borders quickly closed. Fear, selfishness and enmity, long abroad in some places, submerged or incipient in others, have waxed or erupted.

We've been hit by cyclones as well as storms, and the damage and danger increases daily.

The more torrential the rains, the more the waters rise: *obviously*. Buildings have been evacuated, with more and more people moving to the hills: rowboats and dinghies being mobilised.

The cliffs are still considered out of bounds. Haunted, as they say. *But why?* Was the philanthropist killed there? The body would have to have been dismembered and the remains hidden under rocks. Would the townsfolk really have resorted to this?

Having gathered what food and drink I can, and bought myself a tent and a dinghy, I'm abandoning the town while it's still possible. However, I doubt that the hills will be safe for much longer. Accordingly I'll take to the cliffs.

Struck by lightning, waves, terrible winds – the buildings are collapsing. The sea has broken through barriers; sandbags have proved of little or no help. Landslides are destroying the hills, and the earth tipped into the sea has caused the water to rise further and further. Screams, prayers, curses are heard as buildings turn to rubble and hills crumble, and people are swept into the waves and out to sea.

The wild girl suddenly appears and punches me hard in the face, knocking me to the ground. I get to my feet and in my anger retaliate: I kick her in the ribs and she goes down. Feeling ashamed, I try to help her up but she hits out at me. I'm sorry to say I kick her again. She lies there unconscious.

The baboons chatter, and then shake their heads, as do the orangutans. And then they wave goodbye.

It hits me now: *this* ark is not going to include any humans at all.

A dove flies over. I look up just as it shits.

They've left: walked off into the distance. I've followed, as stealthily as possible. And I can now see what I was never allowed to see before. I'm taken aback by the sheer array of animals – far more diverse and numerous than I'd supposed – and by the size of their vessel. How long did it take them to build it, for God's sake?

Though I don't really think they will notice, I wave back to them as they disappear into the Barque.

PURSUIT INTO SALT

Having broken away from them, I ran... faster than I'd ever run before; in spite of the many bruises and pains from the beating they'd given me.

No, I'd never trusted any of them, and I hadn't gone with them willingly.

Punched and kneed; repeatedly thrown against the school's wire mesh fences; kicked when I fell; mocked and jeered at: this had been a routine set of occurrences.

And I knew they were fully capable of worse: a tramp had been caught and kicked to death by some of them, far out on the playing field. No charges had ever been made, as no proof was presented.

R. was one of the ringleaders. He seldom did any violence himself, and in fact he sometimes affected friendliness. But I knew that he incited others.

He had the sort of glint in his eyes that has nothing to do with intelligence – intelligent he was not – and certainly not with anything at all good. Just the opposite: it was a perverse, malicious, nasty and devious little fire that burned there. – More sense of this will become evident. I couldn't imagine him ever really *smiling*, although perhaps he did. A grin, not a smile: that was what stood out.

He wasn't the only one, as I've already said. But he was amongst the worst.

Nor was I the only victim. D., for instance. One of my few friends. He did have rather girlish – effeminate – ways, true enough. That made no difference at all to me: I liked him for the sensitive, good-natured boy he was. The bullying that was handed out to *him* increased considerably after the sports teacher christened him "princess". (Yes, there were bullies – and sadists – amongst the teachers, too.) He left the school when it became intolerable.

Why did those boys hate me? I was never sure. I suppose they needed *someone*, and I fitted the bill: shy, bookish, a bit of a loner; hopeless at sports, apart from running, at which I excelled. And I preferred to run away when I could, rather than fight: this branded me as a coward in their eyes.

I had never told my parents about the relentless bullying, partly out of pride, and partly fear of reprisals.

Never until the other day, at least.

Or perhaps I should say it was discovered, and I couldn't find it in myself to lie about it. The bullies had usually avoided my face. This time they hadn't.

'What happened to you?' my father asked. 'You have a black eye and a bruised cheek!'

'And you've been bleeding!' exclaimed my mother. 'From both your nose and your mouth!'

My father had gone to the school. There'd been heated discussions. My mother had made complaints, also.

Friday evening. My parents and I had gone to the local railway station, not far from our house. I intended to visit D. and stay over with him and his mother, and had an overnight bag with me. While we waited on the platform, a commotion broke out – prolonged shouting and loud swearing – just outside the station.

'You both wait here', Dad said, 'I'm going to go have a look.'

We waited. The commotion continued, and I thought I heard Dad's voice added to it. But Dad didn't return.

'I'll go', said Mum. 'Something must have happened.'

I waited. But she didn't come back.

Instead, R. appeared.

'All by yourself?' he said.

'Where are my parents? *What have you done?*'

'*Your parents?* You mean your *parents* who've made all those com-plaints to the school? How should I know where your fucking parents are, snot-face?'

He grabbed my overnight bag.

'Going somewhere, are we? I don't think so.'

Then the others came onto the platform. I looked around, but there was neither escape nor help – as often the case, the station was desert-ed at that time. I shouted 'Help!' anyway, but it did no good: it just made the bullies laugh.

They shoved, hit and kicked me. One of them tripped me up and I landed hard on the cement platform. I was dragged to my feet, and frogmarched out of the station and across the road. I shouted 'Help!' again, but no one stirred.

It was at this point we heard it: a loud and prolonged bellowing, coming from somewhere near my house. I was taken aback, and so were they – we all stopped, and R. and the other boy who held my arms let go of me.

I seized my chance. I broke from them and ran as I'd never run before – towards my house and, as I thought, safety. It took them little time at all to follow, angrily shouting after me, but I had the advantage of a lead, as slender as it was, and my speed.

Sick with fear and dread, I pounded down the pavement and made it to the front door, around the corner from the main road. Then I remembered: the keys were in my travel bag! I banged the door with my fist, hoping they'd hear and think I'd gone inside and slammed the door shut, and dashed down the street and across the road, then through an alley and down another street.

I had to stop, eventually. Exhausted, shaking, legs aching and heart thumping, stumbling at the last, I couldn't go on.

I saw something move out of the shadows, possibly – I thought – a cat or small dog. It was a koala – a little bear-like creature with brown and white fur, a largish head with a black nose and prominent furry ears. I'd only seen photographs and films of these animals before. – I knew some had moved from the bush into the outer suburbs in search of food, but I could scarcely believe my eyes to see one so near to the centre of the city. Especially as eucalyptus trees – the sole source of their sustenance – were few and far between where I lived.

He padded over to me, climbed up my leg and clambered into my arms, snuggling against my chest.

'You don't want to be here', I said in a whisper as I cuddled him. 'They're vicious, and they're coming. They'll hit you, kick you, kill you – that's what they're like.'

I'd heard of horrible things done to these animals from time to time – for instance, a koala had been hacked repeatedly with machetes and then flung onto a campfire by thugs who were supposedly protecting their dog from the poor creature. I could easily imagine R. and his friends doing something similar, given the chance....

I had to run again. *I had to.*

The koala clung to me as I staggered along – that was all I could do, in spite of the short rest I'd taken, and even then I couldn't keep it up for long. I stopped again, and put the koala down.

Shouts, curses and the sound of running, not far away, made my blood freeze. 'Run!' I said to the koala. 'Please – you have to go! *Now!*'

But he remained sitting there, and, bizarrely, seemed to shake his head.

R. and his companions rounded a corner and began walking towards us.

Suddenly rays of light issued from the koala's small furry body, blinding and burning light, slanting upwards and streaming towards the bullies. Yet the koala itself seemed unharmed. I had to look away, due to the brilliance.

The pursuers had... *disintegrated*: quite literally. I might have thought they'd simply run away, but there were remains on the ground... not ash, mind you... more like *salt*. I walked over and picked a little up, and I'd swear it *was* salt – *hot* salt.

'You're not an *ordinary* koala, are you?' I said.

He looked up at me, and shook his head. Then he scampered away. I didn't try to follow him.

And thus my life came to a close. Or so at the time it seemed. It can still seem like that, on bad days. I'd lost both parents. And I'd witnessed something extraordinary and scarcely believable: deeply haunting and yet... a little bit ridiculous.

Such indelible memories!

My doctor and I sat in silence for a while. By that time the surgery hours had finished: I'd been her last patient for the day, and I was grateful that she'd let me tell her this long story.

'You're a writer', she said; 'you should write about it. It might help.'

'Perhaps', I replied, 'perhaps.'

'By the way, do you drink straight from the bottle or from a glass?' she asked. I laughed, and so did she. I wasn't surprised: she knew about my drinking.

But such indelible memories!

(In tribute to James Sibley Watson and Melville Webber, the makers of the film 'Lot in Sodom' (1933))

Notes

Notes on 'Freddy and Ian, Who Sailed Across the Sea on a Raft'

Freddy is of course right, an antechinus isn't a mouse, though ante-chinus are sometimes referred to as marsupial mice or pouched mice. They're marsupials, not rodents.

The "Ian" of the story refers to Ian Fairweather, a Scottish-born Australian painter, often considered one of Australia's greatest artists. He did indeed cross the Timor Sea on a home-made raft in April 1952, when he was sixty. The raft washed up on the island of Roti in Indonesia, where Fairweather was arrested. Fairweather was sent from Roti to Timor and then to Bali. The impression one gets is that the authorities didn't know what to do with Fairweather, but that they were still suspicious of him. Eventually he was deported to Singapore, where he was placed in a Home for Penniless People. The story becomes even stranger at this point. Richard Casey (later Baron Casey), the Australian politician and diplomat who was married to the artist Maie Casey, tried to arrange for Fairweather's return to Australia. For whatever reason, this didn't work out; instead, he was repatriated to the United Kingdom (he was a British citizen, after all, even if he'd been making his home in Australia). Fairweather had to obtain the fare back to Australia from his relatives.

This in brief is the fairly well known factual story of Ian Fairweather's raft voyage and its aftermath. (Well known to those interested in the history of Australian art and artists, at any rate.) My story places an antechnius named Freddy within the very heart of the story. In this it differs from any official version of these events, such as the one in Murray Bail's book *Ian Fairweather*. You will not find Freddy mentioned in any biographical literature about Ian Fairweather, or indeed about Maie Casey. You might decide that this story is purely a work of the imagination, even if it relates to certain facts. You may even decide that it's entirely fiction, and that "Ian" isn't Ian Fairweather and "Maie" isn't Maie Casey. Or you may decide that an antechinus could indeed have learned the English language, and have been a close friend of Ian Fairweather's. After all, *why not?*

Two further things I'd like to mention:

Freddy's account of Ian's paintings is of course what an antechinus would make of them, not, for example, what an art historian would.

Ian Fairweather did indeed translate a book from the Chinese: it was called *The Drunken Buddha.*

A Note on 'Jay and the Flamingo'

The California-based artist Jay DeFeo (1929-1989) worked on her monumental painting *The Rose* between 1958 and 1966. During this time she was married to fellow painter Wally Hedrick, and her associates included artist and magazine editor Wallace Berman and poet Jack Spicer.

How closely you, the reader, may wish to relate the characters in this story to DeFeo, Hedrick, Berman and Spicer is obviously up to you. Perhaps, instead, you'll regard the characters as entirely fictitious – with the exception of Beatrice the flamingo, of course.

Notes on 'The Mirror of the Fatal Shore'

I thought of calling this narrative 'A Koala Who Was Condemned to Death Has Escaped, or The Wind Blows Where It Listeth', as a homage to the great French filmmaker Robert Bresson; referring to his film *Un condamné à mort s'est échappé ou Le vent souffle où il veut*, known in English as *A Man Escaped*. As I might as well blow my own horn here (no one else is going to, as the saying goes), the reader may like to look at my essay 'Bresson: Cinematography and Personhood', in *Labrys* 9, November 1983 – though I should add that the text contains a number of typographical errors.

But as you can see, I didn't call the story by that title.

"The Fatal Shore" is a phrase from an Australian convict ballad from the early 1800s. Robert Hughes used it as the title of his book *The Fatal Shore: A History of Transportation of Convicts to Australia, 1787-1868*, first published in 1987. I acknowledge my indebtedness to Hughes' book for background information on the colonisation of Australia.

Another book on Australia, Laurie Duggan's insightful *Ghost Nation: Imagined Space and Australian Visual Culture 1901-1939* (University of Queensland Press, 2001), was a source of stimulus, however indirect for the most part, in the writing of this work.

The epigram from Empedocles comes from Kathleen Fraser's *Ancilla to the Pre-Socratic Philosophers* (Harvard University Press, 1948). The phrase "The unfamiliar land" is apparently a reference to the world of human life; I use it to refer to England. David employs an earlier translation, Arthur Fairbanks' (from 1898), to make the same reference. Fairbanks' translation can be conveniently found online, at the following website:

http://history.hanover.edu/texts/presoc/emp.html#book1

According to conventional accounts, it wasn't until 1881 that a live koala made its appearance in England. Clearly this is incorrect: we know that koalas were in Herne Bay far earlier than this.

Herne Bay would have been referred to simply as Herne in the early 1800s. See for example John Clancy's *Herne Bay through Time* (Amberley Publishing, 2015). I should mention that in common with other writers on the region, Clancy does not mention the Herne Bay koalas.

I can't tell you how far David travelled before he reached The River of Time, or where exactly this was. I've been informed that I'd be subject to a law suit by the county councillors.

I will conclude by noting that I have endured, during the writing of this story, criticisms from admittedly well-meaning readers who deny the possibility of koalas acquiring a human language. Such cynicism! The anthropocentric worldview is still very much alive, with all its unfortunate arrogance towards non-human animals.

Notes on 'Lionel's Story'

Frederick Franck's excellent book *Days with Albert Schweitzer: A Lambaréné Landscape* (Peter Davies, 1959), was a useful companion while writing this story. Franck's is both a lively and balanced account of Schweitzer and his hospital, I would say.

The Rilke poem, 'Archaic Torso of Apollo', is widely available in English translation, including online.

Sadness and joy: interestingly, Tunde Jegede says something similar about African music in the notes to his recording *Lamentation* (Triciom Records).

AFTERWORD

by Anthony Rudolf

It is momentarily tempting to raise the Coleridgean notion of suspension of disbelief, that is, of critical faculties, when faced with David Miller's anthropomorphism, or Wittgenstein's thought: "If a lion could talk, we could not understand him". But it would be pointless. David Miller's magic circle of talking animals does not involve philosophical issues of perception. What you read is what you get, the fables of a sophisticated metropolitan intelligence at a slight angle to the universe of his central artistic and critical concerns. Foregrounded here, or fairgrounded, are social and political issues about human behaviour and responsibility towards the Other, which could not be more significant at a time when the developed world is on trial concerning refugees, the Other at the border. Miller unfolds the stories of his creations/creatures (I am reminded of the line in the old slave song "all God's chillun got wings", and not only Miller's Beatrice, a pink flamingo) as they interact with human beings. Complicit, we enter into, we participate in, this colourful world of comedy, tragedy and history just as we enter into and participate in the sound world of a composer or the visual world of a painter. However, with music and painting, the otherness of the medium is self-evident. With writing, it is not, because writing is what we use to talk about the created verbal world of a fabulist such as David Miller. Miller is a conjurer of narrative, pulling not rabbits but koalas, cat, marsupial mouse, flamingo and others out of the hat or from behind the reader's ear. Said ear takes delight in the adventures of this intrepid gang. The animals have a hard time but they come through. As does the reader, entertained, educated and re-humanised by this encounter with the Other.

About Chax

Founded in 1984 in Tucson, Arizona, Chax has published more than 230 books in a variety of formats, including hand printed letterpress books and chapbooks, hybrid chapbooks, book arts editions, and trade paperback editions such as the book you are holding. From August 2014 until July 2018 Chax Press resided in Victoria, Texas, where it was located in the University of Houston-Victoria Center for the Arts. UHV has supported the publication of *Towards a Menagerie*, which has also received support from friends of the press. Chax is a nonprofit 501(c)(3) organization which depends on support from various government private funders, and, primarily, from individual donors and readers.

In July 2018 Chax Press returned to Tucson, Arizona, while maintaining a partial affiliation with the University of Houston-Victoria. Our current address is 1517 North Wilmot Road no. 264, Tucson, Arizona 85712-4410.

Recent books include *A Mere Rica*, by Linh Dinh, *Visible Instruments*, by Michael Kelleher, *What's the Title?*, by Serge Gavronsky, *Diesel Hand*, by Nico Vassilakis, *At Night on The Sun*, by Will Alexander, *The Hindrances of Householders*, by Jennifer Barlett, *Who Do With Words*, by Tracie Morris, *Mantis*, by David Dowker, *Rechelesse Pratticque*, by Karen Mac Cormack, *The Hero*, by Hélène Sanguinetti, *Since I Moved In* (new & revised), by Trace Peterson, and *For Instance*, by Eli Goldblatt.

You may find CHAX at *https://chax.org/*

About the Author

David Miller was born in Melbourne (Australia) in 1950, and has lived in the UK since 1972. His recent publications include *Spiritual Letters* (Series 1-5) (Chax Press, 2011), *Black, Grey and White: A Book of Visual Sonnets* (Veer Books, 2011), *Reassembling Still: Collected Poems* (Shearsman, 2014) and *Spiritual Letters* (Contraband Books, 2017). He has compiled *British Poetry Magazines 1914-2000: A History and Bibliography of 'Little Magazines* (with Richard Price, The British Library / Oak Knoll Press, 2006) and edited *The Lariat and Other Writings* by Jaime de Angulo (Counterpoint, 2009) and *The Alchemist's Mind: a book of narrative prose by poets* (Reality Street, 2012). He is also a musician and a member of the Frog Peak Music collective.